Dance of Love Copy

Gigi Hodge

Contents

Dedication

To my husband, for everything you do and especially for your two-day trek through mountains, lakes, and jungles to get my new computer!

1

The Date from Hell

Etienne

This has to be the worst date ever. I glanced across the candlelit table at Carol? Karen? I couldn't, for the life of me, remember her name. Thankfully, I wouldn't need to remember because this would be the last time I would voluntarily see this woman again. The date was so tragic that I planned to cross the street if I ever saw her walking towards me on the sidewalk.

"So, I told her that her outfit was completely gauche and last season. Can you believe she had the audacity to discuss fashion with me?" By this point, I thought of her as Cruella. Ignoring my efforts to change the subject, Cruella ranted on and on about the assistant she mistreated, her words dripping with disdain. She sneered, recalling her satisfaction in reducing the poor assistant to tears. Her shrill voice carried throughout the restaurant, loud enough that even the jazz pianist threw her dirty looks.

What was Nanny Clothilde thinking? I mean, yes, beautiful and successful. She met *those* criteria, but I'm pretty sure I told Nanny that my top criteria were that they be kind and fun-loving. This wench was the opposite of those essential criteria. I focused on Cruella again. She was silent, and I wondered if she had asked me a question.

"What?"

"I asked you, Eddy, if have idiots like that at the Sheriff's office. It's probably why you want to move on to the FBI." She cut and bit into her bloody rare steak. Blood droplets trickled from the corner of her mouth. I motioned with my napkin, but the vicious little vampire ignored me.

"Actually, the Sheriff's office is full of brilliant, hard-working people. And the name is Etienne. Just say these three letters, 'A, T, and N'." I frowned at her. "Who told you I wanted to join the FBI?"

"Your nanny, of course. I told her I didn't want some public service loser ... Well, I said that I wanted someone ambitious. That's when she said you were conditionally accepted into the FBI and that you would head to Quantico right after Christmas."

Note to self, tell Nanny Clothilde less about my life.

"Well, I approve." She finally wiped her mouth with the napkin.

Goody, I thought, but did not say. Because my nanny raised me right.

"So, once you join, will you go to New Orleans, or perhaps New York?" She focused on cracking her lobster claws, so she missed my grimace when the juice splattered everywhere.

"Cru ... uh ... we don't get to select. The FBI assigns us. It's not unlike the military. They tell us where to go and we go." Between the lobster spray and the blood, I had lost my appetite. I placed my napkin on my plate and took a healthy swig of the Châteauneuf-du-Pape wine.

"You can't select?" She asked and then chowed down on a big hunk of lobster claw, dripping in butter. Her chin glistened with butter. I wondered if the Swiss boarding school she attended had just given up on teaching her manners, or were they too intimidated to broach the subject?

"No. I can't select."

"In that case, I don't think we can keep seeing each other," she said, still chewing on lobster.

Thank God. Keep your mouth shut, Etienne. Instead, I nodded my head and said, "I understand."

Wiping her mouth with her napkin, she tapped her glass for more wine. "I need someone who's going places, but I need to know where that is. Thanks for dinner." I glanced down at her plate. She had ordered the most expensive meal on Charlie G's menu, a surf and turf with an aged ribeye. Getting rid of Cruella was worth every cent. Nevertheless, if I ever allowed Nanny to set me up again, it would be for a coffee and not a steak dinner.

Before Cruella could leave, I saw a flash of red at the corner of my eye. Gelly Landry, my friend Beau's kid sister, popped up beside our table.

She greeted me with a cheerful grin on her face. "Well, hey there stranger!"

"Hey yourself!" I answered, smiling back. "How was Canada and your year-long *séjour* in Paris? *Tu parles français asteur?*" I asked to see if she spoke French now.

"*Bien sûr! Qui c'est ça?*" She nodded and motioned with her chin to Cruella.

I shrugged, pressing my lips together. "J'ai oublié son nom." [I forgot her name.]

"*Terrible!*" Gelly chuckled.

"Excuse me! Some of us don't speak your countrified French. I only speak Parisian French."

Gelly rolled her bluish green eyes and switched to an authentic Ile-de-France (Parisien) accent. "*Je m'excuse Madame. Si j'avais su que vous parlez le vrai français. Je n'aurais jamais osé de parler ma langue telle quelle.*" Gelly looked at me and crossed her eyes. I coughed to cover my laugh.

"What?"

"Yeah … that's what I thought. Hello, I'm Angelle Landry and you are?"

"Caroline Dupuy." Caroline brushed her silky blond hair behind her bare shoulders.

"*Enchantée.*" Gelly extended her hand to shake, but Caroline ignored it.

"What did you say?" Caroline asked, annoyed.

"You sure you speak French?" Gelly tilted her pixie head and asked her.

"But of course." She said in English with a fake French accent.

"Wow! So, I just wanted to say hi to Etienne. I'll let you get back to your … date." As she moved, her burgundy hair brushed aside, showing the scars on her face and neck. Caroline pushed back from the table; horror etched on her face.

"Oh my God, what's wrong with your skin? Is that contagious? You look like a monster!" Gelly folded her arms in front of her and scowled at Caroline. Then turned her attention to me.

"Wow again. *Tu l'as trouvée ayoù?*" Gelly rolled her eyes, asking where I found my lovely date.

"Nanny Clothilde." I shrugged.

"Nuff said." Gelly shook her head and turned back to Caroline. "It was lovely to meet you, to listen to your non-existent French, and to have you insult me. I think I will head out, though."

"Are you going to let her speak to me like that?"

"Excuse me. She did not insult you, you insulted her. You insulted her language and her looks."

Caroline flipped her hair over her shoulder. "They needed to be insulted."

With that, I threw down my napkin. "Okay ... this date is over. I'm getting an Uber to take you home. I can't stand another minute with you."

"I don't know why I agreed to this pity date to begin with."

I glanced over at her empty plate. "I'm just gonna guess, but perhaps to get a $70 steak dinner."

"And cheap to boot."

"I'm not averse to spending money on a date. I'm just averse to dating cruel, arrogant, and self-centered people. You know what? Get your own Uber. Vaurien." Because Cruella was without doubt a useless human being.

"What did you say?"

"I said your French sucks." With that, I threw a wad of cash on the table to pay the bill. As I left the restaurant, I'm almost certain I heard applause.

2

Sunday in the Park

Angelle

After mass, I was taking a break from the constant scrutiny and gossip. I skirted around the giant live oak on the side entrance of the church. The kids were already climbing the tree as their parents had coffee and donuts and chatted in the community room adjacent to the church. Deciding to walk around the Meauxville town square, *Le Carré*, as they called it, I thought it was time to start planning for my dream. I called my best friend and cousin Renee as I walked.

"I'm gonna do it," I said without a greeting.

"Excellent. With whom?" Renee snarked back.

"You're hilarious. I mean the dance studio." I crossed the street and looked to my left. A heron was fishing on the bank of the Bayou Teche. On opposite sides of the street were the Little Big Cup Restaurant and the Académie French Immersion School.

"Good for you! You've been talking about that since before you got married," Renee said.

"Is it bad that I can only do it because of Alex's life insurance? Am I profiting from his death?" I crossed the street and headed into *Le Carré*.

"Don't be silly. Alex would be thrilled. He would want you to do this. He's been gone nearly two years, Gelly. You're allowed to move on with your life. So, where, when, and how can I help?"

"I'll let you know, maybe someplace in *Le Carré*, I'm looking now and I'll keep you in the loop. *Bisous.*" I kissed into the phone.

"Right back at ya," Renee told me and hung up.

Scrunching my nose, I examined this first side of *Le Carré*. It included the *La Grocerie*, an empty storefront, and the rowdy bar, Cowboys. I had no desire to lease a place next to a bar. I crossed the street and walked to the next side of the town square. It started with the Sheriff's satellite station. Next to that was an empty storefront, two in fact, and also Soleil Café. Other than that, no businesses were on this side of *Le Carré.* Then I reached the last block of the square. I passed *Vieux Vieux* Antiques, the *Au Bal* dress shop, an empty storefront, and *La Coupe* hair stylist. *Perfect, mothers can drop off their kids for dance, get their hair cut, shop for clothing or antiques, and get a coffee.*

I put my forehead against the window and scanned the interior of the space. *Perfect size and perfect location.* Decision made. I noted down the phone number on the 'for lease' sign. Smiling, I walked through the Acadiana Park under the weeping willows and crepe myrtles to the gazebo in the center. *Ahh peace,* I thought as I settled myself in the gazebo at the center of the park. Once settled, I unpacked my after-church snack of healthy muffins and a thermos of black coffee. I cocked my head at the sound of footsteps and bit my bottom lip. Like most dancers, I instantly recognized people by their gait.

"Would you like some coffee, Etienne?" I asked as he climbed the gazebo stairs behind me.

"How did you know someone was behind you, and how could you tell it was me?"

"Were you trying to sneak up on me?"

"I was trying to apologize for my awful date's behavior, but I was going to make my presence known once I got closer."

"Hmm, I saw a BBC Future special on Brit Box that talked about how blind people can tell when people are looking at them. They said there are other clues that our senses pick up on that we attributed to a sixth sense, but it's really the regular five." I didn't turn to look at him when he climbed the gazebo stairs. I just kept focusing on that empty storefront between the *Au Bal* clothing store and the *La Coupe* hair stylist and imagined my studio there.

"How could you tell it was me?"

I kept my focus on the storefront but answered him. "You create a specific rhythm when you step. Most people do."

He sat down beside me and followed my gaze. "Whatcha looking at?"

"Did you know I quit my job?" I kept envisioning my studio.

"A non sequitur, but no. Does this have something to do with that empty store front you're staring at?"

I nodded. "One goal that Alex and I envisioned together was saving up for my dream of opening a dance school. I majored in dance in college. I love dancing."

Etienne put his arm around the back of the bench behind me. "Your dance at Beau and Shell's wedding was amazing."

Smiling, I turned to him. He looked adorable in a bronze Adonis kinda way. "Dancing has helped get me through these past two years. It's also helping me heal by keeping me healthy and making my skin more supple."

"I'm glad. You look healthy."

With a sigh, I examined the building again. "But change is hard."

"I hear you. I'm heading out soon. To get trained at Quantico."

I rolled my eyes. "I know, everybody knows."

"How does everybody know?"

Clueless man. "Your Nanny Clothilde. That's how."

Etienne rubbed the back of his neck. "She's killing me. According to her, her health is failing. Because of that, I had to promise her I'd find that special someone before she passes. Personally, I think she'll outlive us all, but I promised."

I chuckled and handed him a muffin and the thermos cap full of coffee. "So that's why you were on the date with what's her name?"

Etienne cupped his hand over his forehead and sighed. "Let's just call her Cruella and yes, for my sins, I must now date whoever they set me up with until I find that special someone."

I snorted. "Cruella, that's apt. Well, at least they don't look at you as if you're a glass doll about to be shattered into a million pieces."

He grabbed both my shoulders and turned me gently to face him. "You're one of the strongest people I know, Gelly."

"Tell that to my family! Do you know they take turns visiting me every day so that I won't be alone? I need to move on with my life, but they keep pulling me back. That's why I'm looking at the storefront."

"Explain."

"They think I quit my job because I was mourning. In part, that's true, but really, I'm a new person. I need a new life. That's why I traveled to Canada and after to France. New life, new language, and now a new profession. I want the profession that I originally wanted in college; I want to dance." My eyes stayed focused. I was envisioning my studio.

"Professionally?"

"No, it's too late for that, and I don't think I'd have been that good, anyway. My dream is to start a dance school ... right there." I pointed to the empty storefront. We sat in silence, looking at the storefront, enjoying our snack.

"This muffin is weird, but delicious." He took a big bite.

"Banana nut blueberry made from oats and almond flour."

Etienne swallowed before he spoke. "Like I said, weird but delicious. So, what's holding you back from starting your dream? Money?"

"No, Alex had life insurance. I could buy the building if I wanted." I had my three bites, so I put the muffin down.

"Then what?" He picked up my unfinished muffin and raised his eyebrows. I nodded, and he dug in.

"It just seems like so much. Like it would be hard to handle by myself. It's not as if I'm not independent, but my independence was about smaller things. Does that make sense?"

"One hundred percent." More silence followed. "I could help you," Etienne said.

I crossed my arms over my chest. "I don't want your charity."

"Good, because you would be helping me as well. I've gotta get the *tanties*—aunties—and my Nanny Clothilde off my back. I need to focus on getting into the FBI and I can't do that if all of my free time is taken up with tragic and useless dating."

As I cocked my head to the side and sized him up, I asked, "What're you suggesting?"

"I'll trade you one date a week, for five hours of labor, to help you get your studio up and running."

"Seriously!?" I grinned as I envisioned the needed renovation timeline changing from months to weeks.

"I'm serious."

I scratched my chin as I gazed across the street. "What about Beau?"

"What about Beau?"

I cuffed him on his shoulder. "Don't be daft. He's my brother and your good friend. I don't want him to get all protective and mad at you. He is in ultra protective mode right now, vis-à-vis me."

Etienne didn't even flinch. He just leaned back on the bench and scanned the park. "I'll let him and, of course, Shell in on the secret, but no one else. I can't deal with another date from hell like that last one."

"Cruella?"

"Exactly, save me from the Cruellas of the world, and I will build you shelves, install mirrors, hang those bar thingies, and we'll be even-steven. Deal?" He held out his hand.

My head swiveled from the storefront to Etienne's extended hand and back to the storefront. I grinned and extended my hand as well. "Deal! Your first task is to help me speak with Mr. Thibodeaux, the owner. He is old school and, from what I hear, he doesn't enjoy dealing with women for business matters. I need your testosterone."

Etienne shook my hand. What's more, he leaned over and kissed my cheek. "Sealed with a kiss. I can help you with Mr. Thibodeaux right away. I work late shift tomorrow and Tuesday, so see if you can schedule something before lunch on either day, and I'll be there."

"Excellent."

"And for that, I'll take you to dinner on Friday night. Where do you want to go?"

"You mean I get your help and a bunch of meals out of this too? This is the best deal I've ever made."

"This will be fun, Gelly. You'll see. Less stress for both of us and some delicious meals with people we actually like. How about we start locally, to get the gossip going parish wide? *Café des Amis* for dinner and Myran's *Maison de Manger* tomorrow morning to create our plan of attack?"

"Sounds perfect," and I kissed him on the cheek. Then I packed up my left-over snacks and walked away.

"Perfect," Etienne murmured to no one in particular, as he finished his last bite of muffin.

$$3$$

Phase One of the Plan

Etienne

Gelly met me at Myran's *Maison de Manger* for breakfast to plan our approach. Her big smile, her bright hair, and her sparkling blue-green eyes stunned me for a moment.

"You okay?" She nudged me on my shoulder.

"Just happy to see you. Glad you didn't chicken out."

Gelly snorted at that and found an empty table for us. As soon as we sat down, Stella came to take our order. With her dyed blond hair and extra make-up, she was a fixture at Myran's.

"I'll have an egg sandwich and coffee, please. Any chance you have wheat bread?" Stella just glared at her. "I guess not. Egg sandwich, please."

"Egg O'Myran and coffee for me."

Gelly kicked me under the table and mouthed, 'Tater tots.'

I bit my cheek. "Can you add some tots?"

"Sure thing, Deputy. Coffee is free." Stella turned back to the kitchen.

"I'm off duty."

"Doesn't matter," Stella said over her shoulder as she walked away.

Gelly pouted. "I never got free coffee as a social worker."

"Perks of the job." I winked at her.

Stella reappeared with coffee. She smirked at me, and I was certain Stella would be updating Nanny Clothilde about this breakfast date. *Good.* When Stella walked away, no doubt to call my nanny, I took a couple sips of my coffee and turned my attention to Gelly. "So, what is the plan for today?"

"Well, I emailed Mr. Thibodeaux, the landlord for the dance studio space. He is meeting me ... us, at the dance studio at ten."

"Okay. What do you need me to do?"

"Well, I need you to make sure he's giving me a fair price. I spoke to the owners of *Au Bal* and *La Coupe*, which are the same size and configuration as the space I want for my studio. They're paying $800 per month. That includes all maintenance, but there were also stipulations as to the changes that could be made."

"So, you need to pay $800 or less, and you want to ask about the renovations you will need to make?"

Gelly pulled out a notebook and turned to a rough sketch of the layout. "Yes, the floor is hardwood, and that works for me, but I need to resurface it to make sure it has a clean, dancing surface. I want to add mirrors to this front area, because ... dance. I also need to drill barres into studs in the wall along these walls here. Finally, if the layout is like *Au Bal* and *La Coupe*, I'll need to frame out two dressing rooms in this back area."

I pulled the notepad from her hand and scanned her basic sketch. "All that seems like work I can help you with, although I'll get Beau to help with it as well, since he's a better carpenter."

"Fine, but don't tell him about it until I sign my lease. I don't need him to do the full court press, trying to pressure me to go back to my old job and give up my dream."

"A sports analogy, look at you." Gelly rolled her eyes, sipped her coffee, took a deep breath, and leaned back in her chair, crossing her arms across her chest. "Ok, *ix-nay* on the *ease-lay*. Your brother will not hear a word about the lease from me."

"Thank you. Also, I'm impressed with your pig Latin. What do you need from my end of this deal?" She grimaced as she took another sip.

"Thanks, I'm no linguist, like Beau, but I make do." She snorted, and a warmth flooded over me. I shook my head and continued. "Well, to make this look real, we need to start with the official first date at *Café des Amis*. I have it all arranged for this Friday at 7:30. You just need to let me know where to pick you up. The more public, the better."

"How about outside St. Francis? I light a candle there for Alex every Friday. Although, I'm usually a little down afterwards. I won't be in a dating headspace."

"That's fine because," I glanced right and left, leaned forward, and whispered, "it isn't a date. I'll park in *Le Carré*, after which I'll find you, and we'll head to *Café des Amis*."

"Excellent. No pressure then. I'll try not to be bitchy." She set her coffee aside and nibbled on her sandwich.

"Bitch away, I'm just there for a fantastic, stress-free meal." Draining my coffee, I gestured to her rejected cup. Gelly nodded, and I grabbed up her coffee as well, grateful for the additional caffeine.

"Should we do other couple activities?" Gelly asked.

I shook away the inappropriate vision of Gelly in bed and asked, "Like what?"

"I've been with one person for the past 15 years. You've been the one dating. What are other dating activities you've done?"

"Other activities?" *Don't go there, Etienne.*

"Haven't you gotten past the dinner stage?"

"Nope, dinner and," I lifted my eyebrows and admitted, "sometimes bed." I grinned with my best cat-with-cream grin and took a long swig of coffee.

"Not on the menu!" Gelly crossed both hands in a stopping gesture to emphasize.

I chuckled. "Good thing because Beau would probably kill me, not to mention, your parents, Mr. Herman and Ms. Denise. They are practically family. You know better than me. What do serious couples do?"

Stella interrupted and set our meals on the table. "Anything else?" she asked.

"Just a warmer on the coffee, that's all, *merci*," I told her. She nodded and set our bill in front of me. Gelly reached for it, but I snatched it away.

"What do you think you're doing?" I held it out of reach.

"Trying to pay for my breakfast?" She dug her wallet from her purse.

I shook my head. "Not how it works."

"So, you're going to pay for all my meals?"

"If we're together, yes. That's how it works."

"Maybe in the 1950s." Gelly snatched one of my tater tots. Then she took some ketchup and doctored it up with spices and sauce at the table: Tony's seasoning, salt, pepper, and Tabasco. It looked delicious.

"I'm sorry. Who's this charade for?" I asked as I dipped one of my tots in her ketchup concoction.

"Your nanny, Clothilde." She ate her perfectly seasoned tot and hummed her approval.

"Clothilde, hmm ... kinda an old-fashioned name." I quipped, canted my head, and gave her my best 'sweet eyes' as I took a big bite of egg.

"Fine, you pay in public and I'll pay you back." Gelly reached over and took two more tots from my plate. She took her time savoring each tot, afterwards she took a miniscule bite of her sandwich.

I grinned as I watched her eat, at the same time, I swung my head in a no. "Not gonna happen, but you can try." Changing the subject to avoid a tiff, I continued, "So, we meet with Mr. Thibodeaux later today. I'll make sure you don't get overcharged and after that we can discuss the renovations you need me to help you make. Anything else?"

"Not today. If all goes well, I'll write him a check and we get the keys today."

Stella filled our coffees back up and winked at me. Gelly rolled her eyes.

Pausing to take another few bites of my meal, I watched Gelly as she played with her food. She took a couple bites of her sandwich, but she kept eyeing my tots.

"You want another tot?" I asked.

She sighed, "No, I already had three."

I sneaked another tot onto her plate and asked, "So, back to our pre-bill discussion. What other activities does one do in a committed relationship?"

"Well, I've only had the one. Alex, as you know, was my high school sweetheart. So, my view of activities might be skewed towards adolescent activities."

"I know. It was like you two were always a couple. Anytime we had family events or trail rides, Alex would talk about you. He was such a goner, even in high school. Never looked at another girl." Gelly started tearing up. "Shit, shit ... I'm sorry, Gelly. Please, don't cry!" I panicked and tried to hand her my napkin, but it dropped on the floor. I reached to pick it up and conked my head on the table.

"Sixty-eight, sixty-seven, sixty-six ..." Gelly counted backwards in French. At that instant, our eyes met, and she covered her mouth with her hand to hide her grin.

"What are you doing?" I asked, rubbing my head where I'd whacked it against the table.

"If you count backwards when you're about to cry, you can stop the tears."

"Really?"

"Honestly. It makes your brain switch from the emotional section to the logical mathematical area. It's also helpful when your friend makes a clumsy fool of himself in an effort to get you to stop crying. Anyway, it was sweet of you to remember how much Alex loved me."

"So, you're, okay?" Gelly nodded and took a deep breath. "I'm fine. Okay, ideas for committed relationship activities. Sometimes we would *trainer*. You know, drive about until we saw a good spot to stop and make out."

"I'm up for that!" I grinned.

"Again, that would be a no. Hmm ... we would go to festivals together. Also, parades like the Christmas on the Teche boat parade, and the Independence Day boat parade."

"Well, between now and when I leave for Quantico, we could go to Festivals Acadians et Créoles and the Christmas parade on the Teche."

"That actually sounds like fun. Also, because I love to dance, Alex would take me to dance events."

"Dance events? Now, those I know next to nothing about. Are there any dance thingies coming up?"

Gelly picked up her phone and scrolled through it. "Yes, at Louisiana University. 'State of *La Danse*' will happen in about a month and, at the Howard Theater, the Alvin Ailey dance company show starts in November. And finally, if I can get you to take me—"

"—You can." I popped my last tot in my mouth and leaned back in my chair to finish my coffee.

"I've always wanted to see Shen Yun. They'll be in New Orleans at the Saenger right before Halloween."

"I'm not sure what that is, but I will get us a suite to spend the night. Separate bedrooms, of course." I put some cash on the bill for Stella.

"It's a Chinese dance troupe that integrates aerobatics with their modern and traditional dance. It's supposed to be amazing, and I've always wanted to go." Her face brightened just thinking about it.

"Then you will go." I handed the bill and the cash to Stella when she came by.

"Yay! This is going to be fun!" Gelly did a little wiggle in her chair and tittered.

My heart thumped a little harder, and I felt warm. *I'm just content that Gelly is happy. That's all. Nothing more.*

"Yes, all fun and no pressure." I finished the rest of my meal, minus a few more tater tots that Gelly stole.

4

The Dance Studio

Angelle

"Well, I don't know about that. What do we need a dance studio for in Meauxville?" Mr. Thibodeaux scratched his thinning gray hair. He resembled a Cajun Bob Newhart.

I rued my red hair because I could feel myself turning bright red with rage. I kept it together, though. "Do you have a granddaughter, Mr. Thibodeaux?"

"I do. A pretty little girl, Claudette, cutest little thing."

"Well, if she is anything like my niece, Bailey Marie, she loves dance. Bailey Marie goes to dance school in Lafayette. Her mama works all day, after which she has to drive all the way to Lafayette for her dance classes."

"Bailey Marie Hebert?"

"That's the one. Smart as a whip and sassy too," Etienne said.

"Why, that's one of Claudette's friends. They go together to that French school."

"Bailey Marie is my niece, and that is one reason I wanted to open this school. So, they can stay in Meauxville and learn to dance. Look!" I pulled up a video of Bailey Marie's first recital.

Etienne joined in, catching on to my ploy. "*Cher*! *Adorable*! I'll bet your Claudette wants to learn to dance too."

"Plus," I was on my game now, "dance helps girls with their self-esteem and their posture, and keeps them healthy."

Mr. Thibodeaux looked me over. He stared at me and my scars. "You that lady that saved the Heberts?"

"I helped."

"Um hum ... Nine hundred dollars a month, with your first and last month, up front." I beamed, knowing that was just the starting bid. *Step one in my dream.*

"Seven hundred and fifty dollars and Claudette gets free lessons for a year."

"Make it two years, and you've got yourself a deal." Mr. Thibodeaux put out his hand, and I shook it. I wrote the check right there. "When do you think the school will open?" Mr. Thibodeaux asked, putting the check in his pocket.

"I'm hoping in less than a month. Need to get a Christmas recital ready for the 'Christmas on the Teche' event."

"Claudette would make a pretty Mary!"

"Now, now Mr. Thibodeaux. We already made our deal. All parts will be earned, but I promise Claudette will have fun."

"I'll hold you to it." He looked around. "Let me know if you need a hand. I'm telling Claudette about her dance classes. You should go to the schools and tell them about your program. They could have the school bus drop off the kids like for karate."

I beamed at Mr. Thibodeaux as he handed me my soon-to-be studio keys. "You're a genius! Thank you! I'll let you know if we need a hand and when classes start."

"You do that." Mr. Thibodeaux headed to the door, and I turned and hugged Etienne.

"We did it!!"

Etienne heard Mr. Thibodeaux at the door. "*Faux pas perdre ta jolie rousse*," he said, telling him not to lose his pretty red head.

"*J'suis pas encore sa rousse!*" I answered back, reminding him I wasn't anyone's red head.

Mr. Thibodeaux considered Etienne and shook his head before he left. "And she speaks French. You a goner, son!"

"Talk about!" Etienne grabbed me up and spun me around.

After Mr. Thibodeaux's departure, Etienne walked around the space taking notes while I measured the space in dance steps.

"It's about six grands jetés long."

"Seriously, us Americans will do anything and use any measure to avoid the metric system," he quipped.

"Hey!"

"Just kidding. How about we get some coffee at Soleil Cafe and work out the logistics? Let me get some standard measurements since I don't think I can go to Guidry's Hardware or Ashy's Building Supplies and ask for boards that are measured in grand jetties."

"Grands jetés." I flew across the floor doing six grands jetés leaps in a row from one end of the room to the other. Etienne watched as I did some more turns, slides, and jumps. I was listening to music in my head and daydreaming as I danced around in *my new studio*.

When I finished, he continued. "Accurate measurement. Still gonna need something boring and standardized to purchase materials."

"Can we go today? When do you go on shift?" I bounced, tugging on Etienne's shirt.

He chuckled at my glee. "I'm free all day. My shift starts at 8 pm until tomorrow morning at 6 am."

"Ugh! Through the night."

"I volunteered for the shifts, so I can give you some help this week."

"Etienne, we met for breakfast at 8 am. Did you only get two hours of sleep?"

With a casual shrug, that was one hundred percent Etienne, he said, "I can sleep once we get your studio up and running. C'mon, let's get some café au lait and a slice of pecan pie and talk renovations."

"I'll have the coffee and a few bites of your pie."

"You can have whatever you like. After you." With a flourish, he held my studio door open, kissed my cheek as I passed, and locked my studio with my new keys.

We walked the half block to Soleil Cafe. Aurelie, the shop owner and my sister-in-law Shell's best friend, greeted us as we entered. "Sit where you like," she told us with a smile and a wave.

Once seated in the cafe, I pulled a fancy notebook embossed with gold leaf with an attached pen out of my giant colorful bag.

"Fancy, is that a Phoenix?" Etienne nodded towards the notebook.

"I thought it was à propos, get it?" I said, pointing to my scarred face.

"You're rebuilding from ashes, so it works, and that is a gorgeous fountain pen!"

"I like pretty things."

"Me too!" Etienne grinned, but lost his smile when I blushed and covered my scars. "What's wrong?"

"Nothing, just a reminder that we are fake dating and I'm not the kind of woman you would actually date."

"Why wouldn't I actually date you? Aside from your brother killing me, you would be a perfectly acceptable date."

My hand brushed the scar on my face. "I'm not pretty."

"No, you're gorgeous. The scar is nothing. Trust me. I have scars like you, both visible and invisible. It's just life, Gelly. No one expects you to be perfect, and if they do, screw them. Now, use your fancy notebook to make an inaccurate, not-to-scale rendering of what you want in your studio, and I'll get us some coffee. You want yours black, like at Myran's, right?"

"Yes, yucky black, but can you order a large skinny pumpkin spice latte for yourself?"

He grinned. "Of course. Pastry or that pecan pie we talked about?"

"Nothing for me, but you can get something, and I'll sample a few bites." Etienne snorted and left to get the coffees and what I hoped would be an extra-large pastry.

When he came back, he continued the conversation. "Normally, I hate sharing anything with anyone, but somehow with you, it feels right. Plus, it's a hoot that you won't order 'bad for you' food, but gobble up bites out of mine."

On his tray he had our coffees and a Nutella-stuffed croissant that Aurelie had suggested because she had sold out of pecan pie. My eyes darted to the pastry.

"Wanna bite?" he asked, grinning because he knew he was tempting me. I had lost a lot of weight since Alex died. Maybe our 'dates' could get me back to normal. I bit my lower lip.

"Maybe a bite or two." I took a huge swig of my fancy coffee and ripped a small corner of the croissant off. "Thank you. Here's my rendering." Etienne looked at the sketch. While not-to-scale, my sketch showed the areas that I deemed most important. Clearly, the dance space and the dressing rooms were tantamount to the project.

"Okay, and I have the actual measurements here. Can I use your journal?" I hesitated in handing it to him, but finally relented, and he created a more scaled rendering for my approval. "Can I rip out a sheet for the list of materials?"

"Absolutely." As he drew and made his list, I took one more bite of the croissant and moaned as chocolate and fat rushed through my system. When he was done, I took his rendering and scribbled my notes on it. "So, we need mirrors on both sides, and we need paint for the walls. Just paint for the dressing rooms and the studio space."

"It's cheap to paint, and it protects the walls, plus it's only like an hour more to finish painting the entire space," Etienne suggested. "First, we need to rent a sander, next we'll need to varnish the floors, and finally we will need a buffer." He took a sip of coffee and a bite of the pastry. "Mmmm."

"Right! It's so yummy!"

"You want some more?"

"Just one more bite." I took a swig of my coffee and continued. "Shell has one of those buffer things at the school we can use. We can rent it from her and support the school." I broke off another piece of the croissant, slipped it into my mouth, closing my eyes to savor its flaky, chocolaty, hazelnutty goodness. Etienne cleared his throat and dropped his fork.

"Okay ... uh... ahem, we need those rail thingies—" He was staring at me oddly.

I titled my head to the side "—You mean the ballet barres. Do I have chocolate on my face?"

"Ah ... no. Ballet barres, we can make them out of thick dowels, but we'll need to sand and varnish those as well." He took a deep gulp of coffee. "A large dressing room outside of the bathroom space. Do you want that separated as well for boy/girl spaces?"

"Hmm ... can you create a way to put a curtain? There tend to be fewer boys than girls in dance, particularly in small towns ... gender norms, you know." I sipped my coffee and again made another mewl of pleasure.

Etienne cleared his throat. "I can do that. I'll use some hooks, chains, and dowels to create a place where you can put up a curtain. At that point, you can choose the curtains you want. If you don't need to divide the space, take down the curtain, and you'll have one big dressing room space." Etienne scrawled out a long list of materials based on my notes and his more precise measurements.

I bit my lower lip. "Looks like a lot."

"Not too much, and materials are not really what is expensive in renovation, it's the labor. And you get that for free. Here, take the last bite."

"You sure?"

"Positive." Etienne leaned back in his chair and watched me savor the last bite.

The trip to Ashys Building Supplies was entertaining for Etienne. I did a little happy dance each time we discovered a fixture or element I loved. We paid Ashys extra to deliver all the in-stock materials to the studio the next day. For the rest of the materials, the Ashys would deliver them the following weekend, ensuring that the bulk of supplies arrived when Etienne was off duty and could devote more time to the project. Etienne drove us back to *Le Carré* and helped me out of his truck.

"Looks like we're ready on my end," Etienne told me as he held his hand out to help me get down.

I grasped his hand and beamed up at him. "Smooth sailing from here."

"Not quite. We have one more obstacle," he said as he guided me across the street to my beat-up VW bug.

I unlocked my car door and turned back to him. "What?"

Etienne propped his hip against my VW and crossed his arms. "I'll give you a clue. It's big, protective, and a retired Marine."

"Ugh ... can't we just let Beau think we're dating like everyone else?" I plopped down in my seat and gazed up at him.

Etienne smirked. "If you don't mind me coming in black and blue."

My eyes widened. "Why would he hurt you for dating me?"

"I think your big brother might assume I'm not serious since I've never dated anyone seriously."

"Never?"

"Nope, and he knows it. Couple that with your delicate state."

My left eyebrow climbed. My eyebrows were thin and the same color red as my hair. Objectively speaking, with my alabaster skin and fine features, I kinda looked delicate, but Etienne was wise enough to keep silent on that topic. Annunciating each word, I asked for clarification. "My ... delicate ... state?"

"Mourning widow."

"For Pete's sake, I might be sad sometimes, but I'm not made of glass."

"The reality is not really gonna keep me from getting the stuffing beat out of me. Also, I think Marc and Armand would probably join in ... we might need to let them know as well."

I threw my hands up. "Why don't we take out an ad in the paper?"

"Really, we just need to keep the truth away from my tanties and Nanny Clothilde. Otherwise, I'm not worried."

"Well, I am. I need everyone to see that I'm not a delicate wilting flower and that I have moved on with my life. I need this subterfuge as well."

"Subterfuge, nice *mot juste*."

"Thanks. Now, go talk to your Krewe. Just let me know how it goes."

"If I'm still in working condition, I'll see you tomorrow. Want me to pick up breakfast from Myran's again?"

"Go to Soleil. I want a bagel. I mean, I'll get a skinny coffee and a fruit salad, and you should get a bagel with all the fixins." Etienne grinned and shut my car door for me. I rolled down the window. "I will do that. I might even get two." He kissed me on the cheek. "*À demain*."

"*À demain*, although I might walk over and make sure you're still alive after your chat."

5

A Difficult Conversation

Etienne

My longtime friends and I named ourselves the Krewe of Roux. Krewe after a Mardi Gras social group. And roux because we often got together to cook and eat (roux being the essential ingredient for gumbo, a mixture of flour and oil cooked until brown). We were outside grilling, standing around an open pit fire and enjoying some microbrews from down the road at the Bayou Teche Brewery.

"Watcha drinking, Beau?" I asked him, trying to start the conversation on a common theme.

"*Loupgarou* Stout and you?"

"Swamp Thing IPA. I like it. It has a bite like your werewolf one. I wonder what their secret ingredient is."

"We might need to ask them. We're all going to have pizza at the brewery this Saturday. Y'all want to come?" Beau asked the entire Krewe. Armand and Marc both gave that plan the nod straightaway. Their pizza was legendary. Beau turned to me.

"You can make it?"

With a nod, I took a sip of my beer for some courage. "I can. I'll be on call and need to leave early, but first I wanted to discuss something with you."

"Is it about how much time you're spending with Gelly? Because we wanted to discuss that with you as well." Beau crossed his arms over his chest, and Armand and Marc flanked him. *Oh crap, the cat is already out of the bag.*

"Yes, so," I hedged. "We're not really dating, but we're trying to make it seem like we are. It seems to be working."

"What, she's not good enough for you?!" Marc 'The Shit-Stirrer' Richard asked.

"What!? No! She's too good."

"Damn Straight!" Armand said.

"Explain, now!" Beau demanded. He stood with rigid shoulders and a locked jaw.

I flipped the burgers and stacked them on a plate. "Absolutely, but let's dress these burgers first. I want your hands occupied and your blood sugars stable."

"This does not bode well," Armand stage whispered to Marc, whose subsequent cough sounded suspiciously like a chortle.

Once we were eating, I explained, "Last weekend, I had the date from hell, Caroline Dupuy. My Nanny Clothilde has made me promise that I will find *the one* before she passes. With that promise, I also had to promise to go out on dates until I found her. A codicil, if you will, to the initial agreement."

"Caroline Dupuy is hot!" Marc said.

"Yes, but she's also a grade A bitch and even insulted Gelly when she came by the table to say hi."

"And she's still alive? I would have thought Gelly would have savaged her," Armand said.

Beau pursed his lips. "She has been off her game since—"

"—No, she wasn't off her game. She gave a subtle insult about Caroline's manners and left with a guarded insult in French about Caroline's supposed French fluency. It was hilarious.

Anyway, I saw her after church eating lunch and decided to apologize to her. She started talking about how everyone," I stopped and glared at Beau, "was treating her like an invalid and just wanted her to restart her old life. She doesn't want that."

"What does she want?" Beau asked.

"To dance and to teach dance."

"That's not a career." Beau rubbed the back of his neck. "She had an excellent job with benefits and a pension."

"That's not what she wants, Beau."

"She doesn't know what she wants. She's still in mourning."

"Gelly may still be in mourning, but she danced her entire childhood and majored in dance at Louisiana University. She and Alex were saving up so she could quit her job and start a dance school. Now, she has his life insurance. What do you think my cousin, your brother-in-law, would want for her, Beau? To keep a job that she hates, or to do what they were planning and saving for. It's Alex's last gift to her."

"Crap, Etienne, you're going to make us cry like little—" Armand hesitated, casting a worried eye at the opened window and revised his statement, "—babies."

"Nice save, Armand," Shell yelled out the opened window. Beau's new wife had bat-like hearing and retaliated at the slightest whiff of sexism.

"Ears like a bat," Marc muttered.

"It's my wife's superpower and a very useful skill when you have four kids or run a school, trust me. Now, back to my sister. Explain the deal."

"It's simple. She'll pretend to be *the one,* so my tanties and Nanny Clothilde will stop setting me up on hellacious dates. In exchange, I'll help her renovate the dance studio that she just rented downtown. By the way, I also volunteered y'all to help out next weekend. I'll be working there on my time off when I'm not taking her to nice dinners and events that she wants to see."

A hush fell over us as Beau contemplated the plan.

After a moment, he asked, "So you're not using her for another notch on your bedpost?"

"Gross, no, and I don't notch my bedpost. I'm not a neanderthal."

"Gelly gets her studio, free labor, and to be treated like a queen when you take her out," Beau commanded. It was a statement, not a query.

"Absolutely, like a queen. I open doors, I send her flowers, we're going to a bunch of dance shows."

"Sounds like love. You're sure to fool Battle Axe Clothilde," Marc said.

"Hey, that's my nanny you're talking about."

"Meanest teacher I ever had. Don't know how she got me to like reading." Armand added, "She tricked me by buying all those comic books."

"Sounds like she had skills," Shell yelled out the window. Marc laughed and mouthed, 'bat ears', pointing to the window.

"Shell," I called back. "Can Gelly talk to your students, maybe do a little dance show for them to see if they're interested in dance? She plans to offer classes in English and French."

Shell zoomed out the door, drying her hands on her apron, with T-Alex, Alex's namesake, toddling behind her.

"Do you think she would be interested in doing a PE class a few times a week for us? We never did find a PE teacher, but we could use dance as PE. No, don't answer. I'll ask her myself." She picked up T-Alex and ran down the porch stairs. Beau caught her, lifting T-Alex from her arms.

"Easy, slowly please." Shell's eyes shined up at him and they kissed softly.

"No PDA during the Krewe of Roux time!" Armand shouted. Beau kissed her again, this time deeply as he gave the finger to Armand. Then he kissed the top of T-Alex's head.

"Walk!" he told her when she came up for air. She beamed dreamily at him and started walking to Gelly's, followed by the trio of border collies, Paul, Bruce, and Rick, or "The Jam," as they called them, after the 1970s punk band. The abandoned pups had found and protected the Littles (the three orphaned children Beau and Shell adopted). Beau watched her until she got to Gelly's. After the attack, they convinced Gelly to move her tiny home closer to the main house and Beau and Shell's home.

"Something you want to tell us?" I asked as Beau's eyes followed his wife as she traipsed across the lawn.

"What? I love my wife and my children. Nothing to tell." Beau grinned.

Armand whacked him on the shoulder. "I'll be damned. You're fixin' to add another Little to the mix. You horn dog."

"First, that sounds sexist, and second, I'm sworn to secrecy."

"I *am* sexist, I can say that. Aren't you supposed to space them out, Casanova? You talked about waiting three years. It's been less than two." Armand snickered.

"It was an accident that led to a happy secret," Beau said, biting his lower lip and fighting a grin.

"Well, here's to happy secrets," Marc toasted, and we clinked our bottles together. We sat listening to the night. Each lost in our own thoughts.

"I'm heading out," I told them, getting up and heading to my truck. "Tomorrow, I start helping her with the studio renovation."

"Not by yourself, you're not," Beau said, as I closed the door. I waved my hand and nodded in acknowledgement as I drove away.

6

Date Prep

Angelle

"Help! I have nothing to wear!" I rushed into Beau and Shell's house the moment they got home on Friday. "Lend me one of your cute '40s outfits!" Shell had an affinity for dressing like a 1940s pin-up girl.

"Gelly, I'm size sixteen. Nothing I have will fit you."

"Ugh, drat it all! Can you come with me to the *Au Bal* dress shop? I just need to find something nice to wear."

Beau frowned. "What for? It's not an actual date." We both shushed him.

"That's a secret. Children can't keep secrets," Shell scolded, flicking her eyes towards the Littles' bedrooms.

Beau shrugged. "Just wear jeans and a t-shirt. Etienne won't care." I shook my head, and Shell made a 'what can I do with him?' gesture.

"You're useless. He's taking me to *Café des Amis* so we can get tongues wagging. If I show up in jeans, that says we are just hanging out as friends. The least I can do is make an effort."

"It's 4:30 now, Gelly. What time is he picking you up?" Shell asked.

"At 7:30, but I also need to light a candle at St. Francis for Alex."

Beau frowned again, but Shell nodded her head. "Ok, I'm texting Emma at *Au Bal*. Give me your sizes, shoes and dress. I'll also text Jennifer over at *La Coupe* to fit you in for a blowout and make-up." Shell looked up at me. I was frozen in place. "Don't just stand there. Grab your purse and evening lingerie."

"Right, on it." As I scurried home to get everything I needed, I heard my brother.

"Soo ... I guess I'm in charge of supper and on T-Alex duty once Mom decides to bring him back? Thanks for helping my baby sister, Shell." Beau hugged her to him and kissed her cheek gently. "Just don't overdo it."

"I'll just be supervising. No labor involved, plus, it will be fun. Gelly hasn't had a chance to take care of herself like this since the fire. It will be good for her."

Shell was right, but I hated that they still saw me as so frail.

Once we parked on the street in *Le Carré*, I headed to the church and Shell went to the *Au Bal* dress shop.

"First the dress," she told me as she walked away. "When you come back, I'll have three final selections for you to choose from." I saw Emma, the shop owner, greet Shell, as she walked into the dress shop.

"Thanks Shell," I called to her, and she waved back. After, I turned and headed into St. Francis. I blessed myself with the holy water, lit a candle for Alex, and then genuflected before I sat in a front pew. The church was empty, so I talked to Alex.

"Hey," I confided, "I'm going on a date tonight. Well, not really, but it kinda feels real. Please don't be mad." A tear fell down my face. *I can't do this. This is wrong.*

A voice came from behind me. "I'm sure Alex is looking down on you and smiling, Gelly."

"Father Lebrun. I thought I was alone."

"You're never alone, Gelly. Especially not here." He put his hand on my shoulder.

I snorted. "I meant alone from other humans."

"I bet that's hard for you these days as well."

I snorted again and nodded to him. "I thought you were supposed to always be deep and philosophical."

"Hard to do that with the girl I gave a ride to in high school who ruined my seats."

I covered my beet-red face with both my hands. "Oh my God, I mean, oh my, I must have blocked that out of my memory. It was my first period. I thought I was dying."

"It was the first period I had to deal with as well." Father LeBrun shut his eyes. "I imagine that Dr. D'Augereau was a bit bemused when we rushed into his office thinking it was an emergency!"

"I still have a hard time looking him in the face."

"I still can't believe Ms. Denise or some of your friends hadn't informed you about ... that."

"I didn't really have a lot of friends, except for Alex and my brothers. I knew some dancers, but we weren't close, plus we were all athletic and lean. We didn't start as early. Besides, Mama was still dealing with Theo's death. She tried to put on a brave face, but ... you know how it is."

He placed his hand on my shoulder. "So do you."

"Ah, there is my philosophical padre."

"You enjoy your date or whatever it is tonight."

I scanned the church to make sure we were still alone. I had to be honest with Father Lebrun. "It's not a date, not really. Just a friend, trying to avoid his family's matchmaking and willing to help me set up my school."

"Whatever it is, have some fun, Gelly. Take a breath and enjoy the life that Alex helped to save. I think that would make him happiest."

"Ugh, now you're going to make me cry again."

He patted my back. "Not my intention, I assure you."

"Thanks Father Lebrun, Kobe."

"You're welcome, Gelly."

I left the church and walked straight to the *Au Bal* dress shop. *I can do this. This is to help a friend. I'm not cheating on Alex.*

When I walked into the shop, I saw that they had pulled dresses in my size. They were going through them to ensure that they highlighted my best features, which were my bright auburn hair, my peaches and cream coloring with a sprinkle of freckles, and my fantastic legs. As a dancer, my legs were my best feature. Terrible feet, but amazing legs.

"This green?" Shell asked.

"Any green should work with her, but it *is* sleeveless. We don't want her to feel self-conscious, and you know people will stare."

"Oh, I like these sheer, flowy sleeves that cinch at her wrists with satin cuffs." I said, surprising them. Emma did not miss a beat.

"Yes, but you need a shorter skirt."

"You're going to love our selections, Gelly," Shell told me. They held up three dresses. A navy blue mini-dress that would hug my body with a faux turtleneck and tight lace sleeves. A more structured celadon green mini-dress that had the translucent flowy sleeves I liked. The sleeves cinched at the wrists and the dress had a rounded high neck. Finally, a mid-length little black dress with a deep V neckline, a 1950s A-line skirt, and three-quarter sleeves.

"Try them on! Try them on!" Emma, buoyed by her selections, practically shimmied out of her skin. I tried on each dress and loved them all. The black one showed most of my scars, but it was elegant and lovely. I did a little celebratory dance around the dress shop in it. The celadon one did amazing things for my coloring. It only showed a bit of the scarring on my neck. The blue one looked amazing and hid all of my scars.

"You know what, I think I will take all three of them and gradually work up to the LBD as I get more courage. For tonight, I'll wear the blue one."

"I'll ring them up." Emma bounced through the dress shop.

"You look amazing in all three," Shell told me. "Your scars don't detract from your beauty, Gelly."

"Well, that's not what I heard. I still need to adjust a bit, Shell. Give me time."

"I'm just glad you're going out to do something fun," Shell said as she pulled out her credit card and slid it towards Emma.

Before Emma could grab it, I slid the card back to her. "Hey, I can pay for my own clothes!"

"Yeah, well, I'm working on strict orders from my husband. You know how your brother is. Besides, you'll be working for free at my school for a while. So just let me do for you, will ya?"

"Not for free. I'm getting free labor. You're letting Beau get off early to work on my studio."

"Which he would have done, anyway."

"And free advertising for my dance school."

This time, Shell handed the card directly to Emma. "That I would have given you anyway, because all community businesses are supported at our school. Just say thank you, all politely, like you were taught."

"*Merci bien*," I said and gave Shell a kiss on the cheek.

"*Pas de quoi*. Now, onto *La Coupe*, where Jennifer is going to get you ready for your date."

"Who's the lucky guy?" Emma asked. Clearly itching to enter the information into the Meauxville gossip mill. *Excellent, our plan was working.*

"None other than our friendly Deputy, Etienne Benoit," Shell responded.

"Well, well, well! So Clothilde finally chose someone nice?"

I grinned. "No, Etienne chose me himself. Thanks Emma, I will be back to talk to you about the dance uniforms and what you'll need to pre-order."

"Sure thing. Come by anytime." Emma said, but right as the door was closing, she continued, "Looks like Ms. Clothilde's machinations are working."

I tilted my head and frowned at that. "What was Emma talking about?"

"Nothing, I'm sure. Just speculating, which is what you want, right?" Shell said as she walked past my studio and opened the door to the *La Coupe* salon next door.

"Of course." But a hint of manipulation scented the air. I frowned in thought, but Shell distracted me.

"Now, let's get your hair and make-up done up right." We walked over to the *La Coupe* salon where Jennifer Istre greeted us bubbling with hairstyle suggestions for my ginger locks.

7

Date One

Etienne

I got a text from Gelly to pick her up at the gazebo. It felt fitting, since that was where we made our deal. I got out of my classic Dodge Power Wagon and walked to the gazebo. I could see someone small seated with her back to me and assumed it was Gelly. She had always been slight. So small I felt impelled to protect her, but Gelly, she had a spine of steel.

"Gelly?" She stood up and turned toward me, and I froze and nearly swallowed my tongue.

"Holy hell," I murmured under my breath.

"Hey, you. Ready to go? I'm starved." Gelly walked towards me in a navy-blue mini dress with her dark burgundy red hair styled in wavy curls around her face. I was transfixed. "You okay?"

"Ah ..."

"Say something. You're making me nervous. I knew this dress was over the top. It's too much, isn't it? I should have just worn jeans, like Beau told me." I held my finger up to stop her babbling, and the corner of my mouth twitched. Then I motioned for her to do a twirl.

Gelly twirled and smiled. "Not too much?"

"Not too much. In fact, I would say that it's just about perfect. Wow, just wow. You look amazing. This is totally gonna work, and everybody's going to envy me. Ready to ride?" I asked, holding out my hand.

"Yes, I'm starving, like I said." She grasped my hand, and we headed down the gazebo steps and through the park.

I leaned toward her, my lips brushing her ear. "I didn't hear you because I was stunned by your beauty."

She snickered and rolled her eyes. "Oh, ach! That was terrible."

"Terrible but true."

"*Anyway* ... where is your squad car?" She scanned the parked vehicles.

"I'm not taking you on a date in my squad car. I made sure I was not on call for tonight." Then, with a wave, I motioned to my Classic Power Wagon.

"Oh, my God. I forgot about this truck. You hardly ever drive it. I remember Beau and Theo helping you rebuild it when I was in middle school. How come you never drive it?"

"It was built to impress, so it's for dates only. Besides, I live in town and most of the time I'm working and pulling double shifts, so I'm in the sheriff's car or, if I'm lucky, the SUV. But this baby—" and I walked around the power wagon, "—is only used on special occasions, like taking a stunning woman out to dinner. Hop in!" With a flourish, I opened the door for her.

Gelly hopped in the truck, admiring the smooth leather seats and the old-fashioned radio. "Original radio?"

I grinned. "Original everything. I got it running in high school but, after that, it took forever to find all the parts to restore her. What channel do you want?"

"We are in luck tonight; KBON is playing *En Français* volume 1 and 2." She switched the radio on.

"Nice Classic Rock in Louisiana French. I love that station." And the Babineaux Sister's version of Bob Dylan's All *Along the*

Watchtower began. We drove towards the restaurant with Gelly tapping her foot and singing along about the *tour de garde.* I smirked. "You have rhythm, but smart move going into dance and not music."

"Is that a comment on my singing voice? Because I can sing louder." She did, just as she threatened.

We were both laughing when I parked the truck. I ran around the hood and opened the door for her. Gelly looked up at me as I helped her down. "You know, you don't have to do that."

"One, yes, I do and two, let someone do for you just a bit, Gelly. Take a breather every once in a while." She rolled her eyes. "Now take my arm and pretend that I'm hilarious." That made her smile, and she held that smile as we walked into the *Café des Amis* restaurant.

I had made reservations, so the hostess seated us immediately. The restaurant had hired a jazz band for the evening, and they were playing softly in the background. Gelly recognized one of the musicians and excused herself to say 'hi'. She hugged him and I tried not to feel annoyed. *Not a date*, I reminded myself. When Gelly came back, she was grinning.

"Someone special?" I asked, trying not to glower.

"My new piano player for my advanced classes and my adult dance hall classes, Mitch. He's a French immersion teacher at Académie school, but his true love is music. It just doesn't pay all the bills, but it feeds his artist's soul. He is going to come work for me when he doesn't have paying gigs. It's all coming together. Thank you again, Etienne." She leaned in to kiss my cheek.

"Glad I could help." I got up to help her into her seat. With a friendly smile, the waitress arrived at our table, set down glasses of water, and handed us menus.

"You really do go all out when you date. Why didn't Cruella snatch you up?" She opened her menu and started scanning.

"Well, one, because I am in no way, shape, or form attracted to her cutting, caustic cruelty. And two, she did not want me because I'm going away and can't pick my assigned city. It could be New Orleans, New York, or a myriad of other locales."

"Nice alliteration: cutting, caustic Cruella. You don't get a say at all?" She sipped her water.

"We can request, and if there's availability and we fit the need, they may let us go to our requested locale, but there is no guarantee. We serve where we are needed."

In hushed tones, Gelly said, "Hence your desire for a faux girlfriend." At that moment, her stomach growled loudly.

"Exactly, now, let's get you some dinner. For a tiny little thing, you sure get hungry quickly. What looks good to you?"

"Well, the fresh-caught bass filet smothered in crawfish étouffée looks delicious. I wonder why they are redundant about it?" She canted her head to the side.

"Because smothered and étouffée mean the same thing?"

"Yes."

"Because not all the patrons speak French. I'll get the bass and you can have a few bites."

Her smile flashed. "Excellent. Then, I will get the bronzed tuna salad. I'll share that with you as well."

"Salad, yummy." I deadpanned.

"You will like this one, I promise. Also, let's order drinks. Just tap water for me. What are you getting?" She grabbed up the drink menu.

I raised my eyebrows. "What do you suggest?"

"I like ... I mean, you'll like the Bayou Teche Highway 31 beers. Maybe the Ragin Cajuns one or Loupgarou?"

"Beau had the Loupgarou the other day. He said it had a bit of a bite. I think I'll try the Ragin Cajun one. It's supposed to be smoother."

The waitress came by and I ordered for us both, as Gelly sat back and enjoyed the music, tapping her foot and swaying in rhythm.

"So, what do you want to talk about?" I asked, sipping my water and clearing my throat.

Gelly's eyes stayed on the band. "I don't know. I haven't been on a date since I was in my teens."

"So ... who's passing notes to whom in PE?"

With a wide grin, she turned back to me, mischief in her eyes. "I know nothing. Although I can say, without doubt, that Beau and Shell are disgustingly happy."

"Ugh! Change of topic. Gooey makes me uncomfortable. Let's switch to small talk. You ready to work with the Littles tomorrow for Habitat?"

"Yes, they're a hoot. The other day, Bailey Marie asked Valerie what my white hairs meant. She told Bailey Marie that it meant that I was old and I better have a family soon or it will be too late."

"Ouch." I winced.

"Right?! Luckily, Tanner chimed in and changed the subject. He told them that the kid might be a girl and that it's better to live without girls, because girls always mess with your stuff."

"Brave, dumb, little boy." I shook my head.

"I believe they took all of his toys hostage, but he just told them that proved his point." Gelly was in tears, laughing. "I'm so glad they are doing well. I try to hang out with them more often, but sometimes I'm just too sad. They probably think I hate them."

"No, but they know you're sad. I was over there with the Krewe the other day and overheard Bailey Marie ask Shell what they could give you to make you happy. Shell told them time." Gelly took a deep breath and lowered her gaze. "There is no timeline, Gelly. No deadline by which you have to be over your grief. In fact, your grief won't go away. You know that because of Theo. Your world just needs to get larger and you won't rub up against your grief so often."

"Shell's mom, Ms. Ellie Mae, told me something similar once." Gelly looked up into my eyes and gave a teary half-smile. "Thanks Etienne."

"Although ... no crying on the date. That would get back to my tanties and Nanny Clothilde, and I will never hear the end of it."

Gelly snickered. "Deal."

The food arrived, and Gelly stole three delicious bites of the bass with crawfish étouffée while she picked at her salad. She ate only what she called 'the good stuff' with a bite of crunchy vegetables. Once the 'good stuff' was gone, she was finished.

"Can I ask?"

"Ask what?" She said, as she stabbed a piece of tuna, adding blue cheese, lettuce, a tomato, and dressing to the bite.

"About the three bites? You seem to make it a habit of ordering the healthiest thing on the menu while convincing me to order the bad-for-you meal. Once the order arrives, you snaffle three bites of my food. Why?"

"Well, I'm an athlete, so I have to feed my body healthy food. I'm also a *gourmande,* and I love delicious food. Delicious food which is often terrible for me. To balance those two parts of me, I order healthy food but allow myself three bites of the bad-for-me food. If I don't treat myself to some yummy food, I'll end up eating all the good-for-me food only to go back later and eat the yummy food I actually wanted. Can I have a sip of your beer?" I handed it over.

When we had finished our entrée, the waitress asked us if we would like dessert. I looked to Gelly. "Well, I don't want any, but I think my date would like the bread pudding in rum sauce. A double order please." The waitress smirked.

"And I'll have a refill on my water. Etienne, weren't you saying how you wanted to try their Irish coffee with Baileys, Kahlúa, and Frangelico?"

"Was I?" I bit my cheek.

"Yes, I distinctly remember you saying that." This time, the waitress guffawed.

"Then I must have said that, so, for me, the hedonist, a double order of bread pudding and a fancy Irish coffee. For my stoic over there, ascetic water." The waitress bit her lips at the not-so-subtle subtext and left to fill the order.

When dessert arrived, I enjoyed watching Gelly savor her three bites of bread pudding and her three sips of the overly sweet Irish coffee. As the waitress placed our bill on the table, I raised my eyebrow, a subtle warning to keep her from attempting to pay for the meal. From there, I drove a replete Gelly home, walked her to her tiny home, and kissed her on the cheek. I stayed outside, waiting to hear the door lock, and then looked up at the security camera I'd helped install to make sure it was functioning.

On my walk back to my car, I noticed Beau on his porch surveilling like the over-protective brother he was.

"If I didn't know better, I'd think you don't trust me."

He walked down the porch steps towards me. "I don't trust you. Not with Gelly. I don't trust any men with her. It took Alex five years before I started to trust him."

"She had some fun, Beau. Let her have some fun." We walked towards my truck.

"I didn't interfere. I just wanted you to know that I'm monitoring the situation."

"Noted. Now get back to your wife and turn your over-protective tendencies on her," I said, getting in my truck.

"There's enough to go around, I promise." I rolled my eyes, shook my head, and slammed the door of my Power Wagon.

8

Habitat Help

Angelle

The next morning, our entire Babineaux/Landry clan woke early to help at the local Habitat for Humanity house. Marc, Armand, and Etienne met us at the main house on the Babineaux farm for a hearty breakfast that Ms. Denise had prepared. After my required three cups of coffee, I inhaled deeply. It felt normal for the first time in a long time. Then I saw Etienne and smiled. It was somehow brighter than normal. As we ate, Shell entertained T-Alex while Beau went over their plans and assignments for the day.

After giving everyone else their tasks, he assigned Etienne and me to assist Valerie.

"Valerie, you can work on your hummingbird garden with your nanny and *parrain*."

"Thanks, Daddy." She beamed up at him, and Beau's lips kicked up as he ruffled her hair. "It was your brainchild, Val."

"Her brainchild?" I asked.

"Yes." Shell glowed at Valerie. "It was Valerie's idea to create a pollinator garden for butterflies, hummingbirds, and bees. I'm so proud of her." Valerie ducked her head, but she couldn't hide her beaming smile. As her nanny, my heart warmed at my brother's good fortune.

After breakfast, Shell and Beau reluctantly handed T-Alex off to be spoiled by both his grandmothers, and we all packed into our vehicles and headed to the site. Once we'd all arrived and started on our respective tasks, Valerie handed Etienne and me a paper.

"Here is the sketched layout for the garden. I have copies for each of you." Valerie was a 40-year-old in an eleven-year-old's body. "Nanny Gelly, you can plant this end of the garden. Just make it pretty. *Parrain*," she continued to her godfather, Etienne. "You do the middle because neither of us can reach that. I'll do the rest."

"Why did I get such a small plot to garden, Val?" I made a grumpy face.

"Because, Nanny, you take forever when you want to make something pretty. Remember when we painted my dresser? I just wanted it white. You spent three hours adding polka dots and flowers on each drawer and then another hour to rearrange the drawers."

I pouted, my hands on my hips. "You love that dresser."

Valerie gave me a side hug and patted my back. "I do. It's the best. Still, it took foreeeever!"

"Noted. I will try to be faster."

With a vigorous shake of her head, Valerie said, "No, that's why I gave you a smaller plot. You make it pretty, and we'll be faster, right, *Parrain*?"

"Just tell me where to plant, what to plant, and I will do it quickly and efficiently with no questions asked."

"You're a little organizer, aren't you?" I told her.

"I have to be. I have four siblings to take care of, or I will soon." Valerie bit her lip.

"I don't think my brother counts as a sibling, Val ..." I said absently as I focused on planting. When Valerie said nothing,

I lifted my head and examined her guilty face. "Four siblings?" Valerie nodded, and I glanced over at Shell. She was at the edge of the site directing the installation of the two planter boxes from under a parasol, with Beau taking her orders and doing the real labor.

I stomped over to Shell, gave her a big hug, and whispered in her ear, "You sneak, you pregnant little sneak."

"Valerie!" Beau yelled out.

"It just came out!" She yelled back, and he shook his head.

"Sorry Gelly, we were waiting for the first trimester to pass before we announced it to everyone. Plus, I'm a little embarrassed. We were planning to have another once T-Alex got to preschool. He's just starting to toddle around and poof! I'm pregnant again." Shell whispered back to me, "Tante Gelly."

I beamed at them, and pecked Shell's, Beau's, and Valerie's cheeks.

"I get to be Tante Gelly to more Littles!" I called out.

"Yes, but you're my Nanny Gelly." Valerie called back.

"That I am Val, that I am. Thank you for inadvertently keeping me in the loop." Valerie frowned, weighing if that was a good or bad. "I meant thank you for accidentally letting me know what was happening."

Valerie bobbed her shoulders. "No problem, it happens to me a lot."

"Something to keep in mind if you have any secrets," Etienne leaned over and murmured in my ear.

I giggled, and Valerie yelled, "*Parrain* and Nanny are telling secrets!"

"You're one to talk," Beau said, and picked her up in a fireman's carry as she squealed. "Let's get some water for the team."

I watched them go and started arranging my plot again. "He really does love being a daddy."

"He's good at it, too," Etienne said. "What about you? You want kids? Rethinking your 'no children' stance?" Etienne asked while he shoveled and planted around me. We worked silently, planting and arranging, according to Valerie's specifications. The sound of the hammers and saws were a relaxing back beat while the smell of soil and flowers cheered me.

Taking it all in, I hedged, not lifting my head. "Perhaps. What is on the agenda for next week's date?"

"Smooth subject change. I'll pick you up next Saturday at 6 am. Wear your best blue jeans and western shirt over a t-shirt and your work boots."

I turned to look at him, and he raised his eyebrows. "Zydeco Trail ride!!!" I said and did a little happy dance.

Etienne grinned. "I take it you like trail riding?"

"Alex used to take me, and I loved it. I haven't been in so long." I turned back to my plot as memories of past trail rides flashed through my head.

Etienne interrupted my flashbacks. "Still remember how to ride?"

"Pardnah, I was raised on a farm, a *horse* farm. I rode before I walked. This will be so fun!"

He jostled my big floppy hat. "Don't forget the sunscreen!"

"I'm ginger. As such, I always have a hat, SPF 50, and protective ChapStick in my purse. I've learned the hard way to never forget them. I want to avoid reliving some pretty painful past catastrophes." I shivered, remembering.

"In that case, you're all set."

"All set!" I side-hugged him.

Etienne hugged me back, his eyes fixed on something over my shoulder. I followed his gaze and noticed Marc and Armand frowning at him from the roof of the house where they were putting up shingles. I had several guardian angels who thought he might be a threat. He shrugged his shoulders and grinned down at me. I laid my head on his shoulder and sighed. Drawing in an energy and a warmth I hadn't felt in a long time. Inside, a soft voice hummed. *This matters*, it said. I shook my head.

9

Zydeco Trail Ride

Etienne

"You up?" I knocked on Gelly's tiny home door. I peered in the side window. The upside of tiny homes was it's easy to tell if anyone's in the house. The downside was that anyone could easily see if you were home. It was a safety issue I would bring up with Beau. I wasn't stupid. Beau could tell Gelly her home wasn't safe. That would have to be a big brother task. Since Gelly was not inside, I checked the barn.

"Gelly, you here?" I called in as I swung open the barn door. The smell of horses, fresh hay, and manure hit me.

"Back here!" I walked towards her voice and saw her saddle up two beautiful quarter horses. The Babineaux Farm only raised quarter horses. One of them was a beautiful, rare champagne colored and the other a rare Appaloosa.

"I thought we would just borrow some horses from my cousins," I said, moving forward to pet the two beautiful creatures.

"What's the fun of that? Besides, Belle and Bête here need some exercise. They are very social and will love the trail ride." She threw the Appaloosa's, Bête's, reins to me and smoothly mounted Belle. "*Allons. Yippi taille yo kaillé!*"

I swung up onto Bête. "You know there are some academics that believe that expression comes from Louisiana Creole Cowboys, right?"

"Oh, yay! History at 6 am. Need more coffee!" She directed Belle to walk out of the barn.

"*Ti-tchu*," I groused, calling her a little ass, as Bête and I followed her. "That was an interesting tidbit."

Clearly knowing the routine, Gelly said, "Let's get going. It's best if we arrive at the church before we hit too much traffic. Lots of *couillons* on the road." She and Belle trotted down the driveway.

Bête and I hurried to keep up. "I'm an officer of the law, don't I know it!"

We got to the starting point at St. Francis Church in *Le Carré* at eight, right as Saturday morning mass ended. A whole group of riders were already assembled, as well as some horse-drawn *wagons* (pronounced with a 'v' sound in French) that included older folk, music, and coolers of beer. The older men dressed up in their western snap shirts and bolo ties. Everyone else was in blue jeans, a message tee proclaiming their riding club, and cowboy hats and boots. There was the occasional baseball cap.

Gelly and I both sported our "Landry Posse Trail Riders" shirts. Like everyone else, our western dress shirts were stashed for the dance later that night. This wasn't our first rodeo. We all started toward the Landry farm with our entrance fees in our pockets, and bandanas ready to wipe off the inevitable sweat and dirt.

As we approached the farm, another cousin of mine, Reggie, who had been close to Alex, sidled up beside us.

"Gelly! We haven't seen you in a while. How you doin'?" He leaned over his horse and kissed her on the cheek.

Gelly beamed up at him. "Reggie, it's so nice to see you. I'm doing well. I missed this."

"Well, you will always be family, so come whenever you want."

"Thanks. Etienne was kind enough to invite me." She threw me a glance.

Reggie stiffened in his saddle. "Yes, I hear he has invited you to several events," he said sharply.

Gelly tilted her head. "Is something wrong Reggie?"

"No, it's just, well, you got over Alex rather quickly. It hasn't even been two years."

Gelly inhaled sharply, stopped her horse abruptly, and turned her horse around to go in the opposite direction of the trail ride. I turned to follow her, but not before I cuffed my idiot cousin on the back of the head.

"*Couillon*! Do you know how long it took me to get her to start going out and enjoying herself? She left the country for over a year after being cooped up in that tiny house for months after Alex died. You're such an ass." We started arguing with each other until one of our uncles put his horse between ours. I noticed Gelly had left the road. I scanned the area and found her sobbing and hugging her horse beneath a tree. *I'm going to beat the shit out of Reggie.* But Reggie had followed as well.

"I'm a complete *tchu*," Reggie said.

"You are that." I left him and sidled up next to Gelly. I reached out and gently stroked her arm.

"Don't listen to that idiot, Gelly."

She swiped ineffectually at her tears. "Do you think Alex thinks I got over him too soon?"

"Gelly, you haven't gotten over him. That is the whole point of our ruse. You get time to focus on your business, and I get a break from dating. You aren't dating me because you're over Alex."

My Tante Lorraine joined us. "Gelly, what did my fool son say to you?"

"He asked if I was already over Alex." Gelly started to cry again.

Crap. "I'm sorry, Tante Lorraine. I'm going to have to kill your son." I motioned for Lorraine to take Belle's reins and I reached over to grab Gelly.

"C'mere, Gelly." I lifted her onto my lap and held her, my eyes shooting daggers at Reggie.

"Please don't cry, Gelly. I'm an absolute *fils d'putain*," Reggie told her, and with that, his mama, Tante Lorraine, whacked him upside his head.

"Are you calling me a *putain*?"

Gelly laughed through her tears. I handed her a clean bandana from my pocket, and Gelly started to cry again. "Alex always had a clean bandana for me."

"They all do, the entire Landry clan," Tante Lorraine told her. "Show her, folks!" All the nearby men pulled out their handkerchiefs and held them aloft.

"And an army knife?" Gelly asked. Everyone pulled out their pocketknives.

I said, "Rule #9: Never go anywhere without a knife. Heck, we had our knives way before Gibbs' rules." Gelly's lip quirked. No doubt remembering watching NCIS with her brothers and their friends, including me, at home every Thursday night. "Feel better?" I asked.

"Yes, thank you."

"Good thing. Otherwise, we would have left my fool son on the side of the road with no phone and no horse." Aunt Lorraine grabbed Gelly's hand and held it. The instant she let Gelly's hand go, she cuffed Reggie upside his head before she returned to the ride.

"I'm really sorry, Gelly!" Reggie said, quickly wiping his face with his handkerchief.

"I forgive you, Reggie."

"Thanks, Gelly. I guess I'm going through my own stuff."

"Of course you are. Friends?" She held out her hand to Reggie.

"No, not friends, Gelly. Family." Gelly started bawling again.

"God dammit, Reggie," I said.

"No, it's okay," Gelly said, wiping her eyes. "Family," she told Reggie, and squeezed his hand.

"Thank God, I did not relish the idea of walking home from here." Gelly laughed. The sound of her happiness shimmered through my body. Something must have shown on my face. Tante Lorraine noticed and pulled out her cell phone, no doubt, to text the other tanties and my Nanny Clothilde. She moved her horse aside, but not before muttering to her cousin, "The old battle axe's plan is actually working."

Without a stealthy bone in her body, she called my nanny. Gelly and I grinned because she kept her phone on speaker and yelled into it. "Barring my idiot son's interference, I think there's something there," she told my nanny.

"When have I ever been wrong?" Nanny Clothilde responded. Tante Lorraine rolled her eyes. Throughout the day, she snapped various pictures of us. Once, as we were walking around the ranch, I was gazing down at Gelly, smiling at her smile. When I looked up, Tante Lorraine was taking our photo. Tante Lorraine chronicled our whole day, snapping pics while Gelly and I enjoyed the smoky BBQ, while we danced in the sun and dust, and when I assisted Gelly onto Belle for the journey back. The ruse was definitely working. Nanny Clothilde surely believed there was something special between me and Gelly. I just had to remind myself again that it was indeed a ruse.

10

Choir Practice

Angelle

When I got home from the trail ride, I called Alex. I know. I'm an idiot to keep paying for his cell service, but sometimes I just needed to hear his voice.

"Thanks for calling. Leave a message, and if Gelly lets me, I'll get back to you."

I heard myself in the background. "Hey, don't tell them that!"

"Of course not. I wouldn't want people to think I'm henpecked." Beeeep!

The corners of my mouth pulled up as tears ran down my cheeks. "Hey Alex, just a quick update. Your family still misses you. Reggie is having a hard time. Etienne has been really kind. But I miss you, and I'm not sure if I want to move on. Maybe, once or twice, I didn't think about you because I was having fun. Is that okay? I'm confused. About Etienne—"

The message cut off. My messages were always too long.

The next week, I just went through the motions. Etienne and the Krewe kept helping, but they all gave me my space. Etienne asked me out again, but I refused. Luckily, I had the excuse of a girls' night. Shell invited me to go to Cowboys with her and Renee that Friday night.

I looked around as I entered Cowboy's bar. It was still a dive with the smell of stale beer and sweat, but it was our dive. It had been a busy week getting the studio ready, and I looked forward to a girl's night. It had been a really long time since I had hung out in a bar with friends. Swaying to the sound of Hank Williams' *Jambalaya*, I squinted through the darkness and found our table. Shell and Renee were doing something they called Choir Practice. I could dance, but I couldn't sing … at all. I hoped it wasn't karaoke. Shell saw me and waved me over.

"You made it." She handed me a drink menu.

I surveyed the bar for a stage. "We don't have to sing, do we? I love music. I love dancing, but I really hate singing." Shell bit her lips together, and Renee guffawed.

"No, silly, Choir Practice is code for we are going out to drink to forget about the little beasties," Shell said.

"Should you be calling my nieces and nephews beasties?"

"They are indeed beasties, but I was more referring to the school children that we take care of 180 days a year." Shell clinked her glass with Renee's.

"So, it's a teacher thing?" I scanned the chalk menu over the bar.

"Correct, and now that you too are going to be a teacher, you need to be initiated," Renee chimed in.

I looked over from the menu. "Does teaching dance for PE count as teaching?"

"It does, but you also are going to be a dance educator at your studio. It counts. Now, what would you like to drink? We have questions to ask, and you need to be good and sauced when you answer," Renee said, and motioned to the waitress.

I ordered, "An old-fashioned with a cinnamon lollipop, or candy, if you have it." The waitress nodded and left to get our order.

"That is a very specific order," Shell teased.

"I like what I like. What are y'all drinking?"

"Whatever beer is on tap for me. I'm on a teacher's budget." Renee made a pouty face. She was not a fan of beer, preferring *frou-frou* drinks like Lemon Drops or Chocolate Martinis.

"I'll have a Shirley Temple, please, because I am the designated driver." Renee harrumphed at that and made big round belly gestures behind Shell's back.

"Shell, have you announced to the world that I'm going to be an aunt again?" I asked, smiling back at Renee as the waitress brought our drinks.

"No official announcement has been made, and if such an announcement were to be made, it would be made after the first trimester."

"Absolutely, mum's the word!" I made a locking key gesture over my mouth. At this point, the waitress brought another beer for Renee.

"Ugh, I really want a kid of my own," Renee moaned. "What with all the kids I see at school every day, my stupid biological clock is ticking *very* loudly."

"Do you want a husband to go with that kid, cuz?" I asked.

Renee's cheeks flamed, and she snorted. "I do, but it's not looking good. I'm thinking of looking into artificial insemination or sperm donation."

"Pricey."

"Tell me about it, hence the light beer and me staying at the little studio over my aunt's *Au Bal* store."

"How much have you saved thus far?" Shell cleared a space on the table for her journal, so she could jot down numbers.

"Five hundred measly dollars."

"How long did it take you to raise that cash?" Shell asked, prepping her journal for division.

Renee covered her face with her hands. "Two years."

"How much does it cost?" I asked.

"For artificial insemination, a fortune. For simple sperm donation, a little over three grand, but it could take a few tries," Renee said through her hands.

Shell added those numbers to her sheet. Then she did the calculation with a small flourish. "So, you need 10 years to raise the capital for one sperm donor."

"Ouch," I said. "You couldn't just, you know ... get a friend to do it for free?"

"I could, but that would require having to deal with a baby-daddy, and I'm not up for that." Renee took a big swig of her beer.

I finished my drink and signaled the waitress for another round. "On me." I mouthed.

"So, the first drink took the edge off. Hit me. What did you want to ask me?"

Renee slurred, "Whad are your intentionz wit Etienne?"

Maybe another round was a bad idea. "I'm dating him. My intentions are to get to know him."

"We know you are fake dating," Renee stage whispered.

Another round was definitely a bad idea. I scanned the room to ensure that no one overheard. "That's true. But sometimes, it feels like we're actually dating. I mean, he's fun and sweet, and he takes me dancing and even to watch dance performances."

"You sure he thinks the dates are all fake?" Shell asked. "I mean, sometimes he looks at you and it doesn't look like he has platonic plans, if you know what I mean."

"Sometimes I look at him and I don't want him to have platonic plans, but I think it's too soon," I admitted.

"What metric are you basing that assumption on?" Renee put her elbow on the table and her chin in her hand when she asked.

"Umm ... well, on the trail ride this past weekend, one of Alex and Etienne's cousins scolded me for forgetting Alex and dating Etienne."

Renee went from holding her head, to slamming both hands down and causing our drinks to jump. "I'm going to kill 'em! Which one am I killing?"

"Easy tiger," I eased the beer away from Renee. "I think you have had enough. Let's get you a coke." I signaled for the waitress, who rushed over.

"What kind of cokes do you have?" I asked her.

"The usual Coke, Dr. Pepper, Sprite." We looked at Renee. Shell raised her teacher's eyebrow.

"Fine, I'll take a Dr. Pepper, but my threat to the asshole stands." The waitress pressed her lips together and nodded, shaking her head as she left.

"It was Reggie Landry, but you can let him live. He already apologized to me after Etienne nearly beat him to a pulp, on horseback no less."

"I would have paid to see that. Caramel colored cowboys and testosterone." This time she put her chin in both her hands as she leaned her elbows on the table.

"You *are* having issues with your biological clock, aren't you?" Shell teased.

Renee massaged her temples. "So many issues, but back to our line of questioning. Why aren't you really dating Etienne?"

"Because of people like Reggie—"

"—That doesn't matter because they are idiots," Shell interrupted.

"And because I don't want to get hurt again," I finished, because that was the real reason.

"Now we have the crux of the matter," Shell said, as Renee dozed off with her fist under her chin. She rolled her eyes and shook her head at her snoring friend. "I guess it's up to me to tell you—take a chance. Etienne is a good guy."

"I know he is. He's the best. We'll see how it goes."

When I got home from 'Choir Practice,' I sat on my tiny porch gazing up at the big sky. Etienne's face and Alex's face flashed in my head. So similar and yet so different. Not only did I not want to just replace Alex. I didn't want Etienne to be his replacement. Etienne deserved more than that. I deserved more than that. There was only one person to talk to about this. I dialed my phone and waited for Alex's voice again.

"Thanks for calling. Leave a message, and if Gelly lets me, I'll get back to you."

I my lips quirked up as a tear fell.

"Hey, don't tell them that!"

"Of course not. I wouldn't want people to think I'm henpecked." Beeeep!

Taking a deep breath, I left a message. One that would never be answered. Asking what I should do.

$$11$$

The Big Date: Part Un [1]

Angelle

Over the month of September, Etienne and the Krewe completed all the renovations to the *Danse avec moi* studio. I started teaching dance classes in French twice a week as PE with the Académie School students. For the French immersion students, I was teaching them everything that they would see at local dance halls and festivals: from the waltz to the two-step, and also the jive. For my studio classes, I added ballet, jazz, and modern dance to the mix. The classes in French were such a hit that I added an *Introduction to Dance in French* class to my schedule as my first after-school dance class.

Etienne was completely off the hook with the tanties and Nanny Clothilde. They were so busy planning our wedding that they never even thought to set him up with someone as a backup plan. He seemed to enjoy fake dating me. We went out every Friday to various restaurants. We even attended Festivals Acadiens et Creoles in Lafayette together. Our dance skills were a big hit at the main *Ma Louisiane* stage. Etienne could really cut a rug.

And, as promised, he escorted me to several dance performances throughout the state. We went to the *State of LA Danse* at Louisiana University and the Alvin Ailey show at the Howard Performing Arts Center in Lafayette. We even followed the troupe to Baton Rouge the next day as they played at the Manheim Auditorium. As the *pièce de résistance*, we also attended church together, although Etienne could not figure out why Father Lebrun glared at him.

This weekend, we would have an overnight stay in N'awlins, NOLA, *en ville*—New Orleans! Etienne booked a suite, two bedrooms, at my favorite hotel, the Hotel Monteleone. We would start our evening with cocktails at the Carousel bar. He picked me up early Saturday morning, grabbed up my luggage, and nodded at my glaring brother as he unlocked his truck.

"N'awlins, I'm so excited!" I jumped right into the passenger seat. "Shen Yun! I finally get to see it. Can I see the tickets? I've basically memorized the Saenger and I'll know exactly which view we'll have when I see the seat numbers."

"Well, hello to you, too. You're supposed to wait patiently while I open your door, otherwise Beau gives me ever more threatening glares. Also, I can see I'm gonna have to step up my game if I'm gonna get you to notice me."

"I've always noticed you. Now give me the tickets." Etienne handed them over. "Front row center!! Really, these must have cost you a fortune."

He winked, closed my door, and rounded the truck. "I have a friend from the Navy who does security at the Saenger. I got his discount. Surprisingly enough, the show did not sell out."

I buckled the lap belt. "Cretins! People are absurd. Wait, there are more tickets in here. Two shows! You got us tickets to two shows!?"

"Well, the other day, while you were planting flowers at the Habitat house, I noticed you changed your perspective before you decided where you wanted to plant each flower. You would go left, then right, close, then far. I figured if you did it with flowers, you would want to do it with a dance show."

"You're right. Usually, I just get up and pretend to go to the bathroom or get a drink. I like to see the dances from different angles."

He started up his truck and started down the drive. "And now you can. The first show, front row center, is an evening show. The second is a matinée so we can be back before dark. So, first order of business. What do you want to listen to on the trip *en ville*?"

"It's Saturday, Zydeco Day on KRVS." I reached down and turned on the radio. "We can listen to both *Zydeco est pas salé* and *Zydeco Stomp*." Buckwheat Zydeco was playing *Ya ya* when I turned on the radio. "Score!" and I started moving to the music in my seat. Etienne smiled and drove the back way through Morgan City. More time for music and less traffic.

Three hours later, with a few bathroom breaks, we arrived at the hotel at around 9 am. I turned off the radio and sighed. "I thought it would take less time to get here."

With a glint in his eye, Etienne said, "Well, I took the back way and then there were all the bathroom breaks."

"Hey, I have to hydrate!" I said and grabbed my purse and water bottle as the Monteleone valet opened the door for me. I looked him in the eye and smirked.

"Merci!" I told him, and the valet grinned back.

"Hey! Over here!" Etienne interrupted, scowling. I wondered if he was just tired or annoyed.

"Be careful with her." He clicked the keys to open the back cab doors and then tossed them to the valet. "And I recorded the mileage, so no joy riding."

The valet caught the keys in mid-air. "Of course not, sir. Do you need help with your bags?"

"I've got them," Etienne said and opened the back doors to get them out of the cab. I almost missed the byplay because I was peering up at the hotel with its cream, ornate, and old-world façade. The flickering gaslights gleamed as the liveried doorman held open the door for us.

"I love this place! The Carousel bar! Are we going there tonight? Before the show?" It was my favorite bar in NOLA, as much for its specialty cocktails as for its resemblance to a carousel. A bar that spins. How could a dancer not appreciate that? I could strike a pose and it would be like I was in a big music box.

"Absolutely. I also have reservations for us at Pêche."

"Umm smoked tuna dip. That is my favorite restaurant *en ville.*"

"A little birdy told me. Are you hungry now? It's early. I made the reservation for one, but I could call and move it up to an early lunch."

"What? And miss out on shopping on Royale Street? I think not."

"Let's see if we can check in early and then we can tour around, if that sounds good."

"Perfect, it sounds perfect."

We checked in early, freshened up in our separate rooms, and had some tea in the suite's living room as we looked down on the French Quarter. Then we headed out to Royale Street to explore. I was practically bouncing.

Etienne grinned. "I need to bring you to N'awlins more often."

"Wow, I forgot how many antique shops there were here." My head swiveled back and forth. I kept stopping to examine what each shop had in the window. "Alex and I got a number of fixtures and decorations here for our tiny home. They are more expensive than The Bank, where most people buy their fixtures, but the experience here is just so romantic." We window shopped for a few more minutes, trying to stay in the shade. Then I saw the antique jewelry store. "You know you could probably find gifts that your tanties and Nanny Clothilde would love here." I pointed to a jewelry store.

"She's right, you know. Nothing better as a gift to women-of-a-certain-age, than jewelry," said a dapper man from the store's portico.

"You work here?" Etienne asked.

"Nope, my uncle owns the store, but I stand by my statement." He tipped his hat.

"Okay, let's go in, but you," he said, pointing to me, "are picking out all the gifts."

"Excellent, shopping with other people's money." I rubbed my hands together. "My favorite pastime."

The nephew grinned and tipped his fancy Panama hat again and walked off while his uncle greeted us when we opened the door.

"My girlfriend is in charge of getting my tanties and godmother gifts for this Christmas. It's early, but I don't know when I'll be back in NOLA."

"Absolutely, tell me about them ..." Then Etienne and I spent some time talking to Mr. Andretti about them. Once we had made our purchases, we asked Mr. Andretti to hold them until that afternoon. Our next stop was the vintage clothing stores. The windows of the stores looked like the set of *How to Marry a Millionaire* or some other late '50s early '60s classic movie.

"Do you do custom clothing here?" I asked the salesperson at the Trashy Diva Vintage store after having shopped around for a bit.

"Absolutely. Let me get our seamstress and we can talk about what you want," she said, calling over another woman.

"Etienne, do you want to go across the way and have some coffee while we do this?"

"You're kidding, right?" He grinned as he lifted a lingerie set in red and looked it over.

"Fine, I'm size four. Find me something to wear underneath a light green mini dress." I smirked. *How far can one push a fake date before it becomes real?*

"I'm on it!" he said, enthusiastic about his assigned task. In the meantime, the seamstress and I discussed how they could make clothes that worked with my scars. The three dresses I bought at *Au Bal* were great, but I wanted something that would knock Etienne's on his *tchu*. I did not question why that was. When they finished taking my measurements and my delivery address, I paid for the dress and the lingerie that Etienne had chosen. By that time, we were starving.

"Pêche?"

"Yes, please. Are we late?"

"A few minutes, but I called while you were in the dressing room. Once I told the hostess where you were, she agreed that you needed some more time. 'Dressing is an art form on Royale.' Her words, not mine. You will probably have to tell her a little about your dress."

When we arrived at the restaurant, the hostess, Tasmyn, quickly seated us. As we walked, I described my dress to her. Tasmyn dressed in a vintage 1950s dress with chunky pink Doc Martens, pale skin, and periwinkle hair and lips. After she had seated us and given us menus, Etienne turned to me.

"What style is that, Gelly?"

"Pastel goth. You're so behind."

"Not a lot of pastel goths in Meauxville or Saint Parish."

"Not yet," I said. "Anyway, she was sweet. Plus, I really love that dress. White with blue polka dots." I called Tasmyn over and asked to take a picture to send to the Trashy Diva Vintage store and get that dress made to my specifications as well. "I'll call them after lunch."

12

The Big Date: Part Deux [2]

Etienne

I didn't even bother to look at the menu. "So," I asked, "What are you hungry for?"

With a wide grin, Gelly said, "Well, I'm getting the smoked tuna dip. It says it's an appetizer, but if you want some, you'll need to get your own."

"You won't share?"

"Nope, not that."

With a huff of laughter, I asked, "Ok, what else?"

"This salad with mixed greens, goat's cheese, almonds, and figs and—"

"—Water. Yes, I know. The salad sounds good. So, what am I hungry for?" Gelly did not miss the laughter in my voice.

"Well, if I were you, I would get some hush puppies and creamy broccoli aïoli to start, then have the baked drum with mushroom sauce. I love drum, ah hem, I mean, you'll love the drum. Then, as your side, try the Brussels sprouts in chili vinegar." At this point, the waiter had come up and began writing down the order.

"And for dessert, *Madame*?"

"None for me, but he," she nodded towards me, "will have the key lime pie with Chantilly and *crème anglaise*."

The waiter turned to me. "And what would you like to eat, sir?"

"That was my dinner order she gave you. She just wants that healthy mixed-greens salad and water."

"You must be hungry," the waiter said.

"Someone's hungry," I murmured, and Gelly kicked me under the table.

"Would you like something to drink as well, sir?"

I did, but I turned to Gelly. "Gelly, what do I want to drink?"

"*Cambremer cidre* and some water for him as well." She turned to me as the waiter left with our order. "If you hate it, I'll drink it, but I promise it'll be refreshing."

"I trust you, Gelly. So, we'll probably finish here around 2:30. How do you want to spend the rest of the day? We can head back at 4:45 to pick up the gifts and still have enough time to get ready for tonight."

She bit her bottom lip. "Well, I know you probably don't want to do anything with the military, now that you're out of the Navy."

"I didn't leave because I didn't like the Navy. I loved serving. I just have a dream."

"Yes, to be an FBI profiler, I know."

I angled towards her and asked, "So, what military experience do you want to do?"

"World War II Museum? I love that place! I learn so much every time I'm there."

"That sounds fun. If you'll excuse me, let me make a quick call to Nanny Clothilde. I have a great-grandfather buried in Normandy. I visited his grave a while back, but I don't remember all the details."

"Call away." I dialed and put the phone to my ear.

"Nanny, *c'est qui…*?" I asked for all the details and took a plain black notebook with an attached pen out of my back pocket and printed his name: Lieutenant Ulysse Benoit.

She motioned with her chin to my notebook. "You carry around a notebook as well?"

"Mine isn't as nice as yours. Plus, it's mostly for work."

She slid the notebook over and read it. "Your great-grandfather, Ulysse, served in World War II? That's amazing. I wonder if we can find him."

"That, my dear Gelly, will be our quest for the afternoon."

She rubbed her hands together. "Excellent, I love quests."

"Noted. Now don't eat all my food," I said as the waiter placed our appetizers on the table.

As all the menu items emerged, Gelly ate hers and savored three bites of each dish she ordered for me. She even drank three sips of my cider. It was amazingly refreshing. I would give her that.

"Oh, I love drum. That's so good! They must put some kind of wine in the mushroom sauce."

"Would you like the rest?" I asked, grinning when she wasn't looking.

"No, no, I just want a taste." She took the last of her three bites of drum and followed up with three spicy Brussels sprouts. She looked at her half-eaten salad and said, "I'm stuffed. Good thing I didn't order dessert."

"I'll bet you are," I murmured under my breath and wondered how much of my key lime pie I would get to eat. Half, that was the answer.

After lunch, we walked the block to the World War II Museum. Gelly and I went up to the front desk and asked the docent if they could find Etienne's great-grandfather. The docent, an older, white-looking man (one can never tell in Louisiana) with a name tag that said Walt, looked me up and down and hesitated.

"I have an indelicate question to ask first. Do you know if he served as a black man or as a white man?"

"Good question, he was light-skinned like me, from what I've seen of him in pictures, and he spoke perfect French. Let me check." I called my nanny and when I got off the phone I said, "He passed. Also, I know he's buried in Normandy."

"So definitely, the European theater. Let's see if you're lucky and if he's one of the soldier experiences we have. It follows a single soldier throughout the war. If he's one of them, we might ask for some more documentation so we can add about how he passed. What was his name?"

"Ulysse Benoit."

"Let me check." Walt typed on his computer. "He's here!" he exclaimed. Let me call our historian. We waited a beat for the historian to arrive.

"What's up, Walt?" he asked the docent.

"Ulysse Benoit! Stephen."

"Yes, I know. He served as a translator in the European theater and in North Africa. He's one of our soldier experiences. Why?"

"He passed! He passed as white. This is his great-grandson. I'm sorry, son, what's your name?"

"Etienne Benoit. I thought he served in the Navy, like me."

"Oh ... he's military as well. This is so exciting!" Walt was practically shaking.

"You must have the wrong Ulysse. There is no record that he was black," Stephen said.

"Of course not, you *couillon*. He *passed*. He probably registered far from home, so no one would know."

"I'm really not sure," I said, amused by the byplay. I looked to Gelly, who was also hiding her smile. "Would you like to speak with my Nanny Clothilde? She is in her 90s and would know."

"Why would I speak to the person who babysat you? What does that have to do with anything?"

"Stephen, you're a moron. Sorry folks, I told them to hire someone local. A nanny in Louisiana is a godmother and often a family relation of the godchild." He shook his head at me with a 'what can you do?' expression.

"Let me just call Nanny Clothilde." I dialed and spoke to her, letting her know she needed to speak in English.

I put her on speakerphone.

"Watcha need, *cher*?" she asked.

"Nanny, this is Mr. Stephen—"

"—Rechter," the historian interrupted.

"This Mr. Stephen Rechter wants to ask you about my great-grandpa Ulysse."

"Well, not much to say." Clothilde started without waiting for the question, "He signed up *en ville*. I mean in New Orleans, because everyone around here knew he was Creole, and they said all the Black soldiers were going to China and that area. Plus, he spoke French, learned it in school and went to the Sorbonne for a year. He said he translated in Europe and in what he called the Maghreb, Africa, I think. He was very brave—"

"—Miss Clothilde."

"Who dis?" she ordered. I winced. One did not interrupt my Nanny Clothilde.

"I'm Mr. Stephen Rechter."

"Well, I'm Mrs. Clothilde Landry Benoit."

"Oh, oh, he's pissed off Tante Clothilde," Gelly whispered.

"Give me that phone and go back to your books, Stephen." Stephen tried to grab it back, but Walt just stared him down. Stephen did not leave, but he let Walter do what he needed to do.

"*Madame* Landry Benoit, my name is Walter James. It's a pleasure to meet you. I'm so excited that we've learned that one of our soldier experiences here is actually a Creole soldier, right here from Louisiana. Is there any documentation you could lend us? Birth certificates, letters home, really anything. Oh, this is so exciting. Is there any way we could come and collect those documents? We'll make copies. Also, do you know who we could contact about a DNA sample?"

"Ulysse Benoit was buried in Normandy. Because they might not bury him in Arlington, if the family came for the funeral." Nanny Clothilde told Walt and added more to the story as he took her off speaker phone.

Walt took copious notes. "Thank you, thank you, *Merci mille fois, Madame* Landry. Clothilde then." He hung up the phone and handed it back to me. "Your nanny is charming, just charming."

"I've always thought so, in her own, battle axe kinda way."

"Battle axe," Walt chuckled. "Oh, I'll have to tell Clothilde when I go visit to pick up the documentation. Apparently, you can give us the permission to do DNA tests. I'm pretty sure he is who you say he is, but there will be doubters."

"Just a minute, Walt. I should be collecting the documentation and the signatures," Stephen insisted and reached for Walt's notes.

Walt shielded his notes and told him, "Clothilde won't give them to you."

"And I won't sign a paper for anyone but Walt here," I added.

"Excellent, this is going to make our exhibit so much more interesting. Thank you. Here's the card to the Ulysse Benoit experience. You and your lady go and enjoy yourselves, no charge."

"Walt, you can't just give away tickets," Stephen pouted.

"Go back to your books, Stephen. This is N'awlins. Things work differently here."

"They sure do!" Gelly said as we walked towards the train that would start our museum experience.

An hour later, I had a whole new appreciation of my great-grandpa.

Gelly was bouncing when we finished. "He was a hero! That's so amazing. More so since we know more about him. I can't wait to tell Reggie."

"Reggie? Have you been talking to Reggie?" I held the door as we walked outside, hit by the heat and humidity, because even in the fall, it was still Louisiana.

"He felt guilty for how he treated me on the trail ride. You know he's considering the Navy as well? I think he looks up to you." She took my arm as we walked back toward the hotel.

"I'm not that much older than him," I grumbled.

"No, but you're much more directionally oriented. You know what you want. Reggie needs that as well. You should talk to him." She leaned her head against my shoulder, and that was all it took to convince me.

"Fine, but not this weekend. What's say we get the gifts, dress for the show, and then get some drinks at the Carousel bar?"

"Sounds perfect." Gelly beamed up at me.

$$
\begin{array}{c} 13 \end{array}
$$

The Big Date: Night

Angelle

I emerged from the bathroom, in my celadon green mini-dress that was fitted with poofy sleeves that tapered into wide satin cuffs. I felt beautiful. While the collar was lower than the blue dress I had worn on our first date, the long, white, flowing Isadora Duncan scarf I wore with it covered my scars.

Etienne's mouth fell open. "Woah! You look amazing. Did your eyes change color?"

"The color of the dress emphasizes an amber ring around my iris, that's all." I did another spin.

"Well, you look amazing."

I fixed his green and brown tie and scanned up and down his brown and off-white seersucker suit. "You clean up well yourself. Let's go get some libations before the show."

"Carousel?"

"Yes, please."

Because it was early, the bar was not yet full. Still, I wanted to sit at the rotating bar rather than a table. I scooted up on my stool and made sweet eyes at the bartender to get his attention.

"I would like a Carousel Old Fashioned, please," then added, "with extra Toschi cherries."

"A *Vieux Carré* for me," Etienne said. A specialty of the house, it got its name from the French name for the French Quarter. The high-end rye whiskey, cognac, vermouth, and bitters were perfect for a night out.

Once our drinks arrived, we discussed Etienne's great granddad and the show we were about to see. "I learned how to say 'Good job' in Chinese. I plan to yell it out to the dancers after the performance."

"Really? How do you say it?"

"*Gan de piao liang.*"

Etienne grinned at me. "And you're going to yell that out?"

"Of course. I want the dancers to know firsthand that they are appreciated."

"You know Chinese is tonal right, so if you use the wrong tones, you could be saying something completely different."

"Good point. I'll log it into my notes, with the audio from my translating app. That way, I can listen before I yell it out." We finished our cocktails as I cut and pasted the audio file into my notes and practiced pronunciation. Etienne even tried pronouncing the expression, much to my delight. I got up to leave and grinned at him. "We can yell it together!"

With a wry grin, he shook his head. "You're so weird."

"Hey, you're the one dating me," I called over my shoulder as I made my way to the front portico.

"Fake dating," He retorted as he followed me outside.

I murmured, "Feels real to me."

At first, I didn't think Etienne had heard, but then I thought I heard a whispered, "Me too."

Out front was a shiny stretch limo. My eyes widened as Etienne directed me toward the door that a chauffeur held opened for me. When I asked why he rented a limo when we had a car, he said, "For you to remember this night, Gelly. When you think back on tonight, I'm hoping you'll smile, remembering every moment."

Once we arrived at the Saenger, we reveled in our VIP treatment. Etienne had purchased the VIP package because he knew I would want to talk to the artists. He even arranged for a translator to meet us backstage. *Hmm. This feels like a real date.* In fact, I couldn't remember the last time anyone had made such an effort to make me happy. This was not good. Or was it? I fiddled with my scarf and bit my lip.

The ushers directed us to our seats in the front row center. I did my little happy dance, and my cheeks hurt from smiling. "I'm so pumped." Etienne mirrored my grin as he sat beside me. "So, up there is where we'll be tomorrow?" I pointed to the balcony seats he reserved for the matinee.

"Yes."

"Excellent. I get a more focused view tonight and a wider lens tomorrow. This is perfect! Thank you!" I kissed him softly on his cheek.

Etienne looked into my eyes, and we leaned towards each other. Suddenly, the lights dimmed, indicating the show was about to start. He leaned down and kissed me softly in the dark, nibbling on my bottom lip. I deepened the kiss, my tongue playing with his. Etienne inched away gently. Allowing us to recover our composure and focus on the show by the time the curtains opened.

I looked into his eyes and beamed. "This is going to be great!"

"I concur," he responded. I tilted my head and stared at him as the edges of his mouth turned up. Something had amused him. After that, the show began.

After the show, I buzzed around backstage running my translator ragged, asking the artists questions. Asking for them to show me leg positions and arm movements repeatedly. I did the movements myself with their guidance to remember each step. Etienne ended up having to give the translator a big tip. I knew I was in trouble when every time I laughed, smiled, or squealed in delight, I locked eyes with Etienne, and he would smile along with me.

When we got back into the limo, I was still bouncing with energy.

"Best show ever!" I swayed as Kermit Ruffin's *Drop Me Off in New Orleans* played on the limo sound system. Then I started knocking my shoulder against his in rhythm to the music. I was dancing with just the top part of my body as the trumpet and saxophone solos played. Etienne grinned at the limo driver in the rear-view mirror, and I could see he appreciated my solo.

"Back to the hotel, sir?" the driver asked. Etienne looked down at me, and I gave him my best pleading eyes. Clearly in the mood to dance.

"Fritzel's?" he asked me as I started swaying to Poncho Sanchez' *Coconut Milk*.

"Yes, please!"

"Fritzel's please," he told the limo driver. The driver changed direction and headed toward the bar.

"Will you need me to stay?" the driver asked.

"You should come in and dance," I told the driver. "Why wait in a car when you can dance?"

The limo driver smiled widely. His white teeth contrasting with his chocolate skin. "I'm good with that. Just no alcohol."

For the first time in a long time, I felt like I was returning to my never-met-a-stranger, pre-fire personality. I directed some questions to the driver as I danced to *Every Day Is Not The Same* by Carol Fran and Clarence Hollimon. I noticed him mouthing the French words, so I decided to get to know him in French.

"*C'est quoi ton nom?*" I asked.

"*André et vous?*"

"*Moi j'chu Angelle et ça c'est Étienne.*" And that was all it took to form a great friendship.

We danced 'til 2 am, closed down the bar, and decided to do a late-night food run. We headed to Verti Marte on Royale and shared Shrimp Po-boys, Shrimp Creole, and some of Grandma's boarding house meatloaf. By the time André dropped us off at the hotel, it was nearly dawn.

"Give me your contacts, André." I handed him my phone so he could do just that.

"Promise me you'll come to Meauxville for our Christmas recital. You have to see how I add some Shen Yun dance moves into the show."

"I promise," André told me. Etienne left him an enormous tip as well.

"I don't think I can remember a better evening. One thing about you, Gelly, your joy is contagious, and you are definitely a people person."

I danced to the elevator, making the concierge and the receptionists smile. "We love this town!" I shouted, only to be met with applause.

While waiting for the elevator, Dr. John's *Basin City Blues* came on. I moved toward Etienne and put my left hand on his shoulder and my right hand in his and we danced. My flourishes and kicks were met with more applause.

Etienne's whisper tickled my ear. "I'm pretty sure we missed our elevator. We've missed it a few times, but I refuse to shut down a joyous Gelly, because that is a thing of beauty."

I fell then. I danced around him as someone turned up the music and some other couples joined us. When the song finished talking about finding heaven on earth in Basin Street, I twirled into him and lifted my lips to his. He crushed his mouth down on me. When we came up for breath, I said, "Screw the elevator. Room. Now." We scurried up the stairs to the strains of *Give It Up* by Gypsy Second Line.

14

Crescent City Crescendo

Etienne

Breathing heavily after having sprinted up the stairs to get to our room, I cradled Gelly's head in my hand, turning her around and crowding her against our room door. I leaned down and kissed her tenderly, nibbling on her lower lip. Gelly, impatient, wrapped her leg around my waist and pulled me close while she deepened the kiss. When we broke for air, I fumbled with the key card as Gelly bit my earlobe. I dropped the card.

"Dammit!"

Gelly smiled against my neck and snuggled closer to me. "What's wrong?"

"I dropped the key."

"No worries." Keeping her leg anchored around my waist, Gelly reached down and grabbed the key. She handed it to me, but I didn't take it.

"Key," she said, and then pointed to the room. "Bed." I blinked and took the key.

"Bendy, I think you fried some of my brain cells."

Gelly laughed, disengaged, and turned to open the door.

Once inside, I pulled Gelly to me and kissed her deeply as my foot swiped the door closed. I slowly unzipped her dress, trailing my fingers over her skin as the dress back parted. The sensation pulled a moan from Gelly. I tried to pull it off, but it wouldn't go down, it was stuck.

Gelly lifted her head. "You tear my dress and there'll be hell to pay."

I tugged again. "C'mon, Gelly, take it off."

She nipped at my earlobe. "I'll show you mine if you show me yours," she teased and started slowly unbuttoning her cuffed sleeves while she stepped back to watch me undress. "You're a Greek statue of a god but fashioned out of Tiger's Eye stone." Once I was free of my clothes, Gelly just stared at me.

"As much as I enjoy your gaze, and you can tell I do," which had Gelly looking down at my dick.

"Impressive," she murmured and lifted her hand to caress me. I inhaled sharply.

"Again, I'm enjoying this," I interrupted, "but you need to reciprocate."

"Dress ... right." Gelly undid the other sleeve, and the dress slid down, revealing the pink lingerie that I had chosen for her this morning. My breath caught and my gaze trailed over every inch of her skin. Gelly moved her hands to cover the scars.

"Don't. You're beautiful," I whispered as I pressed gentle kisses along the trail of scars, from the side of her face to her neck, and down her arm. I traced my lips over her torso, over the hidden scars there. Gelly shivered.

"I can feel the pressure, but not your lips," she said and shook her head, closing her eyes.

"Gelly, we all have scars, inside and out. Look at me."

She shook her head again. "You're *too* perfect."

I barked out a laugh. "Look closer, Gelly."

She opened her eyes and looked more closely. Her head canted to the side. "I thought you were perfect."

"Hah! Not even."

She traced her fingers over my scars. I had scars, lots of scars. She saw one she hadn't noticed before on my neck. She kissed it. "Where did you get this?"

"Fence."

"You fenced? Like *The Three Musketeers*?"

"No, running through a hole in a fence. Some rednecks thought I was acting too big for my britches and wanted to teach me a lesson. When I explained to them that my family had been going to college in Paris, while their families were still working as peasants for aristocrats, they took offense."

Gelly chuckled.

"Hey, I'm supposed to be seducing you, not entertaining you."

"Then you best get to it," she ordered. I grabbed her up and tossed her on the bed. She giggled and reached for her shoulder strap to take off the bodice.

"No, please, leave it on this first time. I have plans for round two." With a gentle push, I eased her down onto the bed, partings her shapely thighs. My hands traced the silk stockings and then the garters, then the bodice that molded perfectly to her pert breasts. I leaned over her, bracing my arms on either side of her. I leaned in and licked each breast through the wispy lace that encased them. Then I nibbled on each nipple until she moaned. As I continued my campaign on her breasts, I shifted my weight to one arm, allowing my other hand to explore her body. From her breasts, my touch traveled down to her torso, then to her belly, until finally reaching her core, where I cupped her.

Gelly gave another telltale moan. I lifted my head from her breasts and took her mouth as I pushed her panties to the side and slid a finger inside her. Her legs lifted and crushed my sides.

I smiled against her mouth. *My Gelly is strong.* As I explored her mouth with my tongue, I pulled my finger out and pinched her clit. Gelly moaned first in pleasure and then in annoyance as I moved away from her.

She lifted up off the bed to look at me and then snorted as I frantically searched my pants for my wallet and then emptied my wallet as I looked for a condom.

"What happened to 'always prepared'?"

"That's the boy scouts, not the Navy. Ah ha!" I held it up in triumph.

"Nice work." Gelly smiled.

"You ain't seen nothin' yet." Without hesitation, I sheathed myself and returned to Gelly. Positioning myself between her legs again, I leaned over her, taking my time as I made my way down her body. I had a system. First a kiss, then a nibble, followed by a soothing lick. After that I blew a soft puff on the wet, sensitized skin, causing Gelly to shiver and moan. Kiss, nibble, lick, puff. I did this all the way down her body.

When my mouth reached her core, I again moved her panties to the side, so they rubbed against her labia as my mouth, tongue, and teeth found her clit. Gelly's entire body shivered. Her legs shook and crushed my ears, and her hands pulled at my hair. As she reached a fever pitch, I angled to the side to allow one hand to come free, and put first one finger and then a second inside her. I wanted to feel her core and her heat as she came.

I rolled her clit between my upper teeth and my tongue. Gelly exploded, her legs crushing my head as her arms flew back. With a few soft licks and kisses, I rose to look down at her. She was smiling softly, her arms and legs akimbo, and when she opened her eyes, I kissed her and grabbed some pillows to put beneath her ass. When I had her positioned how I wanted, I smiled down at her as I entered her. I played with her clit and her breast to elicit some aftershocks and that was all it took to set me off.

"When I wake up, I'm gonna feel guilty for not doing anything," Gelly teased.

"Gelly, you did everything. Now rest up. We're not done." Gelly tittered at that and tucked herself into my shoulder as I drew her to me.

15

Reality Bites

Angelle

I woke up with Etienne spooned against my back, his hand cupping my breast and one of his thighs between my legs. I felt a wave of pleasure and relaxed back into him. Then the guilt hit me. When I straightened suddenly, he woke up. His hand felt so good trailing down the side of me, and that made me feel even more guilty.

"I have to go," I said and moved to get up. Etienne caught me by the shoulders and gently turned me toward him. He saw tears streaming down my face.

"Gelly, what's wrong?"

"Nothing, I just need to go ... go to the bathroom."

He held me firmly and raised his eyebrows. "Really? That's what's making you cry?"

I shook my head.

"What's wrong, Gelly? We both had a little to drink, but we weren't drunk. This was a mutual decision."

"I know, Etienne, you would never take advantage of me. It's just ..." Etienne waited. I could not look at him. I turned away from him and pretended to gaze out the window. "It's just that

I woke up and felt like I had cheated on Alex." Etienne let me go in a flash, as though I had burned him.

"I ... I'm sorry Gelly." He rolled out of bed, picked up his clothes, and ducked into the bathroom to take a shower.

"I'm sorry, too," I whispered to the closed bathroom door. I heard the shower start up.

As though he feels dirty now. Sighing hugely, I packed my things. We still had another show to go and see, but suddenly I felt like a weight was pressing down on my chest. Now I missed both Alex and Etienne. I was just a big mess. After packing everything but my outfit for the show, I fled outside for a walk.

I walked down Royale to the St. Louis Cathedral. Strolling inside, I gazed at the French paintings that told the Gospel. I lit a candle for Alex and then just sat, wondering if I had just ruined one of my closest friendships.

After leaving the cathedral, I walked around Jackson Square and dialed up Alex's voicemail again.

"Thanks for calling. Leave a message and if Gelly lets me, I'll get back to you."

I had to sit down on the curb when I heard his voice. As usual, I snickered at the rest of the message.

"Hey, don't tell them that!"

"Of course not. I wouldn't want people to think I'm henpecked." Beeeep!

"Hey Alex, I did something bad. Only it didn't feel bad and I don't know if I cheated on you. You've been gone for nearly two years. I've kept myself busy with learning French, taking care of Shell's niece, and then starting my school. When you died, I couldn't do anything at first. I just reminded myself to breathe. Now sometimes, my life gets busy and full, and I have to remind myself of you. Am I a bad person? —"

"—We're sorry, but this mailbox is full." I blinked and then panicked. What did that mean? Was it a sign? If so, a sign of what? I dialed Renee.

Renee's phone rang about five times before she picked up. "Hello? Gelly? What're you doing calling me so early on a Sunday?" Her voice was rough.

"Sorry, Renee. Listen. I can't talk to Alex anymore!" I hugged my knees as I sat on the curb.

"Gelly, are you okay? Did you get in an accident? Alex has been gone for nearly two years."

"I know, but ..." I had to fess up. "I've sort of kept his phone on and I send him voicemails when I need to talk to him. It's crazy, right?"

"Not crazy. Tell me what's wrong." I told her about the date, the dance, the ... encounter afterwards, and finally about how I tried to tell Alex, but the voicemail was full.

"What does that mean?" I rocked on the curb.

"Gelly," Renee's voice was gentle, "It just means that maybe you have talked enough to Alex. Maybe it's time to let someone else in. Where are you? Do you need me to come and get you?"

"I'm outside St. Louis' Cathedral. I need to call Etienne. He's probably worried about me."

"Call him but remember that he's your good friend and whatever you decide, he'll understand."

"Here's hoping. See you soon." I hung up on Renee and started to dial him when my phone rang. It was Etienne.

Etienne

When I got out of the shower, I checked to make sure Gelly was not in the bedroom. While I dressed, I called Armand. Clearly, a call to Beau was out of the question. He had already promised to maim me if I hurt Gelly. Pretty sure this counted as hurt. Armand answered with a bleary, "What!?"

"I fucked up, Armand."

"Of course you did. Be more specific."

"I hurt Gelly."

"You, my friend, are attached using an inclined plane wrapped helically around a cylinder ... *autrement dit* you're screwed!" Armand was a big fan of the Big Bang Theory.

"Funny, Leonard! However, my priority now is not saving my ass. I need to fix this."

"Okay. I hesitate to ask this. I don't want to be guilty by association, but what happened?"

"We ... you know. Then this morning, she said that she felt like she had cheated on Alex."

"Ouch!"

"Right! I think it hurts worse because I felt the same way. Alex was my cousin, and I had always been enamored with Gelly. When she was married to Alex, I just admired her and hoped that one day I could find a girl like my lucky cousin Alex. Now that Alex is dead, I feel guilty, like I've stolen her."

"Well, don't tell her that! There's no reason to make Gelly feel bad. Where's she now?"

"I don't know. She left the room."

"New plan. Find Gelly and talk to her. Now leave me alone. I'm sleeping."

With that statement, I scanned the room. She was gone, but at least her bags were still there. It didn't make the panic subside, but it gave me a chance to take a breath and call her cell.

Gelly picked up her phone immediately. "Yes, Etienne?"

"I'm sorry! Can we talk? Where are you?"

"I'm walking off my sad in Jackson Square, in front of the St. Louis Cathedral. I lit a candle for Alex as well, so I'm not feeling as guilty. Catholic scale, of course. We are never without guilt."

I sighed deeply and grinned. "Serendipity, *ma belle*. I already made reservations for us at the jazz brunch at Muriel's."

"Well, that's right here. I love that balconied façade and Muriel's is one of my favorite restaurants. I suppose the least I can do is let you feed me and grovel a bit. Friends?"

"Always, Gelly," I said and grabbed my keys, wallet, phone, knife, and hankie, then headed out the door.

When I arrived at Muriel's, Gelly was at the bar nursing a Bloody Mary.

"Starting early?" I whispered in her ear.

Gelly turned and motioned to the stool beside her. A libation awaited me.

"We have some talking to do, and I figured we would need some liquid courage. Plus, libations for brunch is a staple. I plan to have mimosas with my meal as well. So, talk to me."

I took a deep pull from the Bloody Mary and chewed on the blue cheese stuffed olive. "I love these olives."

"Right back at you, but not what we should be discussing."

Gathering my courage, I rolled my shoulders and inhaled deeply. "I'm not sorry, Gelly. I feel a little guilty too, but I really don't think Alex would mind." Gelly raised a single perfect eyebrow. "I mean, of course, he would have when he was alive, but I never even flirted with you when he was alive. You were strictly off limits."

"I know. It's just a lot to work through. You're just my first since Alex. You're the second man I've ever been with. My whole life it was just Alex."

"I know. I was there."

"So, maybe we got carried away. Maybe I need more time. Maybe—"

"—Whatever you need, Gelly. Just don't push me away. I can wait. I can even try to forget this ever happened. I won't, but for you, I can pretend. Just … just don't go away."

"I'm here. You're one of my best friends. I can't lose that. Let's just rewind and go back to how it was. Can we do that?"

"We can try. I'll try. So, that means we're still going to the show?"

"Yes, but since I ran off, and I don't want to hurry brunch, we'll be dressed a bit more casually."

"Meh ... it's a matinee. That's normal."

We sipped our drinks until the Maitre D' said that our table was ready. After that, we ate their three-course brunch with mimosas for Gelly and café au lait for me. We tried to get back to our old rhythm. It wasn't perfect, but it would do.

This detente lasted through the show until the limo brought us back to the hotel to change and leave for our trip home. When we got in my car and cleared the city, I turned to Gelly and said, "I've changed my mind."

"About what?"

"About Friendsville. I don't want to be there. I'm willing to wait a bit, but I want more than friendship."

Gelly was silent for a while, and I just let her be. She often needed to process and, since there was nowhere to dance in the car, that processing would take time. Having said my piece, it was now up to her. I told my phone to play some Chopin. Gelly couldn't dance, but I could put on some calm music to soothe her nerves and help her process.

When we got to the Babineaux farm, Gelly turned to me. "I'm not sure Etienne. I need more time to think about it."

"I know. Just don't think too long." I got out and rounded the car to open the door for her.

"Then there is the fact that you're leaving soon."

I pulled out her bag from the back seat. "Not until after Christmas. There's still time." I was walking with her, carrying her bag to her tiny home, when Beau appeared out of nowhere.

"Beau!" Gelly said and hugged him. It was a long hug and Beau's eyes narrowed on me. Or maybe I was just imagining it. After the hug, he took a step toward me and then sucker punched me. *Nope, not imagining it.* Gelly yelled, "What the hell are you doing, Beau?"

Beau grabbed me by my shirt collar. "Fake dating my ass. It's all over the internet."

"What are you talking about?" Gelly said, as she tried to get in between us. We both gently pushed her aside.

Shell trotted down the porch steps, pulled Gelly away from the melee by the back of her shirt, and then played the video on her phone. It was our dance in front of the Monteleone elevator. Apparently, one of the receptionists had gotten it on video and the hotel had put it on their social media. There were over a million views. Gelly's first reaction was to smile at the memory, but then she switched her gaze toward where I was standing next to Beau, an enraged Beau.

"Oh, crap," Gelly said, and that's when Beau shoved me to the ground. From the corner of my eye, I saw Gelly sprint towards the back of the house.

Then Beau grabbed my hair and shoved my face into the ground as he yelled at me.

"She's my sister. You can't touch her! You told me you wouldn't touch her!"

"No." I slipped from his hold and rolled away. "I told you I wouldn't fuck with her. That I would never hurt her."

"Well, how do you think she feels now that the whole internet knows you slept with her?" He punched, I blocked.

"I don't know how she feels. We were discussing her feelings when you came up and punched me. We only just learned about the video." Another punch, another block.

"How dare you hurt her!" and with that Beau made to punch me again, but instead swept my feet out from under me. *Fucking sneaky Marine.*

Enough defense. This bastard was going down. I punched, using an upper cut from my position on the ground. Connecting, I yelled, "I'd never hurt her! I love her!"

At that moment, we were both doused with water. We both turned soaking wet to glare at Gelly, whose mouth hung open in surprise. She looked at us both, made a sound of disgust, and then made a beeline for her house.

Beau punched me in the stomach then. "Still looks hurt to me," he said.

Then Shell scolded, "Go and talk to her." Beau turned to go after her. "Not you ... Etienne." And I moved to follow Gelly to her house, but not before I heard Beau whine.

"But, Shell!"

"No. She's a grown woman and based on that dance, I would say that she's making her own choices."

"Bad ones, if you ask me." He raked his fingers through his hair in frustration. *Serves him right*. I smirked as Shell pulled Beau back to the house.

"Luckily, no one asked you. Now come inside and explain to the Littles how you were just pretending to fight Val's *parrain* and how nobody is leaving them."

Beau looked up and saw his children looking anxiously out the window. "Sorry," he muttered.

"I know, *mon amour*, but they have been through a lot and you need to reassure them that they are safe and the people they love ... even if they don't do what you want them to ... will still remain in the family."

"Humph," he grumbled, but walked up the porch steps, gave her a kiss on the cheek and prepared to explain to the Littles that we were just sparring. Yes, that's what we were doing.

"I'm sorry, too." I called after them and waved at the Littles to let them know everything was okay. Then I headed after Gelly.

When I got to her house, Gelly was sitting cross-legged on her porch bench, looking at a picture of Alex.

"I loved him too, you know. I understand the guilt. It's what's been holding me back."

She looked up from the photo. "I'm afraid..."

Moving up her porch steps, I took a seat on her bench. "I'm afraid too, Gelly, but I'm more afraid of losing you. Please give me a chance. I know you need time, but don't push me away."

With gentle kisses, I hugged her close with both arms. Her fingers threaded through my hair. I deepened the kiss and gripped her tightly, pulling her ever closer. The sudden ring of my work phone jarred us apart.

"Sorry, I'm back on call this afternoon." Answering the phone, I listened to the dispatcher. I met Gelly's eyes and let her know what was happening. "I've got to go. It's Ray. He has been spotted back at the Chretien Point Plantation grounds."

Gelly stiffened. Her hand covered her scars. Ray, with the help of Shell's ex-husband, had burned down the Babineaux camp, killed Alex, and left Gelly with scars. Knowing how uneasy she was, I kissed her hard to reassure her. I turned to leave, but I called Beau on speaker as I stormed to my truck; so Gelly knew she wouldn't be alone, and that Beau would be on guard.

16

Le capon [Coward]

Etienne

I rushed to the old plantation site. Two deputies had called in the sighting. Once I got there, I opened my trunk to retrieve my protective vest and scanned the premises for the deputies that had called it in. Their car was there, but they were nowhere in sight. I continued scanning as I called for more backup, explaining that the deputies that made the call were missing. I saw it then, a hole dug into the ground. A small metal box lay open next to it. The sunlight glinted off something metallic on the ground. I reached down and picked up the object; it was an old, rusty, dirt-encrusted key. I slid it into my pocket and continued searching for the missing deputies.

When I scanned the perimeter, I found them lying on the ground. They were both so still, my heart rate picked up. I hurried toward them, kneeled over, and felt for a pulse. They both had faint pulses and clear gunshot wounds in their extremities.

I yelled into my radio. "Deputies down! I need an ambulance and some immediate back up. Faint pulse and clear GSWs to the arms and legs." A twig snapped in the tree, right beside my car, as I was talking. I turned, training my gun on the sound, and taunted Ray. "Really Ray? Attacks from behind or attacking women and children. Is that all you can do? You're a coward."

"I want what's mine!" Ray yelled from the undergrowth, helping me to get a better fix on him. *Thank you very much.* I adjusted my aim.

"Really, and what's yours, Ray? I mean, besides the prison cell that we have reserved just for you?" I could hear the sirens in the distance and hoped they would arrive soon.

"The Hebert's fortune is mine!"

"Hebert's fortune. You've lost your mind. The Hebert's have no money. You knew that when you started dating and then killed their mom. And even if they did have money, which they don't, are you an Hebert?" *This lunatic is mental. That does not bode well for me.*

"That's what you think. I might not be an Hebert, but I'll find that fortune. Finders keepers." He paused, and I knew he was taking aim. I was about to be shot. Before the shots hit me, I got off a couple of rounds and dropped to the ground. Ray's howls of pain were sweet satisfaction as I felt his shots barrel into me. Most hit my vest, but I felt a burning across my arms and my neck. Something was wrong. I tried to stay conscious, waiting for backup to arrive. From the ground, I heard Ray move towards me. No doubt to finish me off. I tried to find my gun, but I couldn't move. I couldn't think. Ray stood over me, his boot on my throat and his gun trained on my head. The gun was shaking, and I stared him down. Ray had only ever tried to kill those that were weaker than him and from behind.

Unblinking, with just a brief flash of Gelly in my mind, I challenged him. "If you're going to kill me, you better look me in the face." I thought it was the end and saw Gelly dancing in my arms. The sirens in the distance became sirens right behind us. As the emergency vehicles pulled up, I saw Ray's boot kicking toward my head. Then blackness.

When I awoke, I registered that I was in a hospital room. I smelled the hospital antiseptic and heard monitors beeping. Doing a quick inventory of my body, I exhaled. My hands and feet moved, and while everything hurt, it appeared that everything was still there. I felt a soft warm weight on my arm. I turned and saw her. Gelly's tear-stained face snuggled against my good shoulder. I turned to the side and lightly kissed her auburn curls. As I kissed her, she moved, and I closed my eyes, savoring the heady herbal smell of her hair that ruffled with that movement. I relaxed back into the darkness, lulled by the scent and feel of my Gelly.

I awoke a second time to a kiss on my cheek. Gelly whispered to me. "You idiot! You could have been killed! What would I have done then? You know what they would have said, right? That I was bad luck. That anyone I love was destined for death. I can't take it Etienne." Then she kissed my forehead. "You have to stay alive and healthy."

I smiled. "Gelly," I opened my eyes and said softly, caressing her face with my good hand. I brushed away a tear with my thumb.

Feisty Gelly returned; her sea-green eyes flashed at me. She moved away, wiped away her own tears, and crossed her arms over her chest. "You were playing possum? What did you hear? Never mind, we'll discuss this once you get out of the hospital. For now, there's a line of tanties and your nanny that want to see you."

"Don't leave, please."

"I'm not going anywhere, you moron. I just need to let everyone know you're awake." Gelly walked over, gave me an avuncular kiss on the cheek, and then quietly opened the door.

"Wait, before the tanties, send in the Krewe."

She narrowed her eyes. "Why?"

"Because I need to speak with them about something." She hesitated for a moment, prepared to argue with me. With a sigh, she nodded. When she trod out the door, I grinned; I was the moron she loved.

A few minutes later, the Krewe came in, confused by my dopey smile.

"Are we interrupting something?" Armand asked.

"No," I sighed. "Does anyone know where my clothes are?" Beau lifted a sealed bag where the ER had stashed my clothing.

"Open it and check my pants pocket for a key," I told Beau.

He reached in the bag, *fouillayed* around a bit, and then pulled out the old rusty key.

"What's that?" Marc asked, reaching for the key. He examined it in the light of the window.

"I'm not sure, but it was next to a box, hidden in a hole, on the Chretien plantation. It might be important. Maybe a safe deposit box? I didn't exactly have time to ask Ray about it before he shot me."

Marc closed his hand around the key. "I will get my PIs on this. I'll let you know when I find out anything."

"Thanks, man. Aside from that, what did I miss?" I asked.

Armand shook his head. "No sir, we have a room of pissed off tanties that were glaring at us when Gelly said you wanted to speak to us first. Now, you must suffer their wrath." Cowards that they were, they fled the scene, leaving me to the tender mercies of some very upset tanties.

17

Faux Fiancée

Angelle

Laying my forehead against the door frame, I collected myself.

"How's your fiancé feeling?" The floor nurse asked, startling me. I scanned the hall to see if anyone had overheard.

"Better, I think. At least he's awake." The nurse handed me a tissue for my tears. "He has a ton of family. Can they go in and see him?"

"One at a time with a maximum of five a day, not including you, of course. He has some deep bruising and cracked ribs from the impact of the bullets. Luckily, he had his vest on. Then there's the concussion." At my cringe, the nurse changed the subject. "Do you want some blankets? You look like a 'I'm not moving until he is well' kinda person. I can make up the couch into a bed once his other visitors leave. Tell them visiting hours are over at 7 pm."

I nodded. "I'll let the rest of the family know they can visit."

The Krewe of Roux were tight with the local LEOs, as they called them, because of Etienne. When one of the LEOs called Beau to tell him about the shooting, I had been lecturing him about the appropriate role a brother played in a grown-ass sister's life. Beau did not have a poker face and caved under my and his wife's pressure to let us know what was going on. I got a ride with him to the hospital and then ran ahead to find Etienne.

When I got to his floor, the nurse said only family could see him. Since no one was around, I told her a little fib. I said that I was his fiancée. Worked like a charm, only now I had a bigger problem. His whole family was in the waiting room, and I was pretty sure I couldn't keep the nurse from blurting out about our non-existent engagement. *I'll explain it all to them later.* I went to tell Tante Clothilde, the Krewe, and the other tanties that he was awake and could see visitors.

In the waiting room, I walked up to my Tante Clothilde, but before I could say anything, Clothilde hugged me. "There, there, *chère*, he's going to be okay."

"I know, the idiot. He's awake and can have visitors, but only five." Clothilde rocked me for a bit and then let me go.

"Let me see for myself. The others can battle out who gets to see him, but I raised him, so I get first dibs." Tante Clothilde swished past me.

"Wait! He wants to see his Krewe first." At my words, the Krewe flew to the door, under the glare of the tanties. They returned in under five minutes.

"Humph," Tante Clothilde said. "It's finally my turn."

"Tell him to stop being so heroic." I called after her.

She turned at that. "Hah! You love that about him and so do we all. You can't get a leopard to change his spots."

"That's what worries me," I mumbled.

"Now, now, you are a good fiancée. You'll take good care of him when he won't take care of himself."

I stiffened. *Seriously, how did she know this already?* "About that—" I said, trying to explain the ruse, but I didn't get a chance.

"—I understand. You just got back from your romantic trip *en ville* and you did not get a chance to announce it. We all saw the video, *cherie*. Don't worry, we understand. Why, you haven't had the time to announce it, have you? We will talk about it later." Tante Clothilde hugged me again, and I nodded against her shoulder.

I raised my head from her boney shoulder and stared into the stormy face of my brother and the curious gazes of the rest of the Krewe of Roux. When Tante Clothilde left to see Etienne, Beau took me by the arm and pulled me into the corner of the waiting room with the rest of the Krewe.

"You didn't tell me you were engaged!" I looked over at the tanties that were gazing lovingly at me. I missed them. They had supported me through Alex' illness and death, and now, they were going to kill me.

"I'm not," I whispered.

"Explain!" Beau did that big brother glare and folded his arms over his chest.

I hissed and scanned the room. "Will you keep your voice down?"

"Beau, it's obvious what happened," Marc intervened. "They wouldn't let you see him, would they?" Tears flooded my eyes as I shook my head. "So, you told them you were the fiancée, and they let you in?" He continued. I nodded. Marc gave me a big hug and told me, "It's okay, sweetie."

I shook my head against his shoulder. Armand took over the hug and held me against his chest. Well, more like his stomach because he was a giant. He, too, tried to assure me. "Etienne's awake now and stable. He's tough and will be fine." I nodded again, bursting into tears, soaking Armand's shirt.

Shell elbowed her way to the center of the group to tug on my arm. "Enough cheering her up already. Y'all are terrible at it." She pulled me to the elevator. "Come with me for coffee and some fresh air." We headed down to the cafeteria. We ordered coffee and an egg biscuit sandwich and moved our trays to the hospital's outdoor patio. I just wanted coffee, but Shell insisted I needed something in my stomach.

Once seated outside, I sniffed my coffee and took a big gulp. I let the scent and the caffeine do its job. Finally, I focused on Shell. "You're lucky, Shell."

"This is true, but in what way do you think I'm lucky?" She smiled and sipped her coffee.

"Beau had already finished his dangerous job when you met him."

Shell's features softened, and she put her hand on mine. "Gelly, you, of all people, understand that even safe jobs don't mean that nothing bad will happen."

I jerked my chin in agreement. "I know. Alex was an accountant. The thing is Shell, I'm not sure I can take something terrible happening to Etienne."

"Something *has* happened to him, and you seem to be holding up." With that, she took a big bite of her biscuit.

"That's because I haven't let myself fall for him."

"Really?" Shell arched her brow and stared me down. "I saw that video too, you know."

With a noisy huff of breath, I pushed my biscuit away. "Fine, but I haven't told him. Thus, I can back away now, before I get in too deep."

"Gelly, I realize this is difficult, but don't make any rash decisions. Let it stew some before you do anything hasty. Perhaps a nice logical pro/con list?"

I scoffed, "That's not how I make decisions, Shell."

"Well, wait until he's well, and after that you could mull it over, maybe?"

A heavy weight settled on my chest, and my chin trembled, but I nodded. "I think I can do that."

18

That's the Job

Etienne

Three days later, the hospital released me into my 'fiancée's' gentle care. Gelly helped me into her miniscule VW and drove me to her tiny house on the Babineaux farm. As she parked in front of her home, she took a deep breath and sat there in the stillness.

Breaking the tension, I asked, "Fiancée, huh?"

Gelly dropped her head and grinned. "Hey, it worked. I broke you out of there, didn't I?"

"I'm not complaining, I kind of like the idea, Gelly." I reached for my door handle, and she stopped me. She shook her head and ran around the VW.

With a flourish, she opened the door for me. "Well, don't get used to it."

I used her shoulders to get out of the seated position, but then kept my hand there and leaned down to murmur in her ear. "Why not? We're good together. You can't say dating me has been hard."

"Well, no..."

I waggled my eyebrows at her. "And I have concrete evidence that you're attracted to me."

"You are such a *trou de tchu*." She hovered as I made my way to her tiny porch. She eased me onto the porch bench and turned back to get the things Nanny Clothilde had packed for me. *Nice escape.*

When she came back to unlock the door, I continued our conversation. "Yes, I'm an asshole, but you still adore me. You can't pretend. I saw your tears."

"You're my friend. Of course, I would cry if you were in the hospital."

"Um hum." *You said you loved me.* But I kept that comment to myself.

"Look, let's get you situated and then we can talk." Once we got my bag in her single bedroom, Gelly turned down the bed and fluffed the pillows. She eased me down on to the bed. *That's the ticket.* Then, instead of lying next to me, or on top of me, she took a second pillow and climbed up to the guest sleeping loft.

"You know, you can stay in bed with me," I called up to her.

"Not gonna happen."

"It happened once," I called back.

"And look where that got us. Beau is barely speaking to me and gives you the evil eye, even as he checks to make sure you're okay."

I chuckled. "Poor conflicted *fils d'*..." Gelly's head appeared from the loft and frowned down at me, and I stuttered a gentler curse, "*Poteau.*"

"I still don't think my momma would be happy that you called her a post."

"Beats the alternative."

Her head disappeared back into the loft. "Or you could stop being mean to my brother and let him know nothing is going on with us."

"I'm not gonna lie to Beau."

"Nothing should be 'going on' with us, Etienne. That's what we agreed to. We had rules."

"It's more what you'd call *guidelines* than actual *rules*," I said in my best pirate cant, channeling Barbossa from the Pirates of the Caribbean. "Sometimes plans go awry and guidelines don't always apply." I began climbing the loft ladder.

"Well, this one won't go awry again," Gelly sniffed. She then held out her hand to stop my progress. Probably for the best, since everything hurt.

I took her hand and kissed her palm. "We'll see."

A week later, I was physically much better, but more frustrated than I'd ever been in my life. Gelly helped me dress, cooked me food, although cooking was not her *forte*, and made sure I had anything I needed. Anything but her. With my sick leave over, I needed to return to work. According to Gelly, I also needed to return to my home, but the thought of leaving her didn't appeal to me.

"Come with me for a late breakfast at Myran's. Let's talk, really talk, but on neutral ground."

"Fine, but I don't think you can change my mind." She crossed her arms over her chest.

"Since I don't know exactly what's on your mind, I have no reason to want to change it. Come talk with me, Gelly."

We got to Myran's. The familiar yellow Formica tables and vinyl chairs felt reassuringly familiar. The place was packed, but the table that we'd first sat at to hatch our plan was available. *Serendipity.* I grabbed the table. Gelly sat before I could pull out her chair. Stella rushed over to the table with menus and water. Ready to serve us and report to my Nanny Clothilde.

"Morning, Stella!" I said.

"Deputy, you're looking well. Looks like Ms. Gelly there took good care of you." Gelly blushed as I responded.

"She took the best care of me. We'll start with coffee, thanks."

"See," Gelly hissed as Stella left, "Everyone thinks we're together."

"That was the plan."

"An engagement was not the plan." She frowned.

I held my hands up. "Hold on! You can't be mad at me for that. I was in a hospital bed *unconscious* when you hatched that plan."

"We can't continue like this, Etienne."

She stopped when Stella brought coffee, and we gave her our usual order. When she left, I suggested, "We could get married."

"Stop teasing."

"I'm not, and I meant what I said when I was arguing with Beau. I love you, Gelly."

She crossed her arms over her chest. "Only you would declare your love for me during a fight with my brother."

"Well, that wasn't how I planned to tell you."

"You had a plan?" She took a sip of her black coffee and grimaced.

I added two creams and two sugars to my coffee and slid it towards her. "Yes, well, it was more of a general outline of a plan. But it involved a more drawn-out seduction, and I was going to tell you once I knew you would tell me back." Gelly averted her eyes and fiddled with her silverware. "But I know you love me. So, I don't need to wait for you to tell me."

Gelly gasped. "How do you know?" She grabbed my coffee and took a sip.

"Actions, Gelly. To make sure I was okay, you took on the whole town and let them think I had proposed, and you had accepted ... including Nanny Clothilde and the tanties. Speaking of which, you don't want to let them down, do you?"

A single tear slid down her face.

"Nope, no crying. Crying is not allowed. I don't know what to do when you cry." I pulled the napkin for her from under my silverware, which clanged on the floor.

She took the napkin, half laughing and half crying. "You can't forbid crying. Crying happens. I'm not sure I can do it, Etienne."

"Do what?"

"Love you that deeply and risk losing you. You have a dangerous job now, if you get into the FBI—"

"—I will."

"Then you will pursue the most dangerous criminals on the planet. I don't know if I can live with the constant fear." The napkin crumpled in her nervous fingers.

"Whether or not we stay together, we'll always be friends, Gelly. Will you worry about me less as a friend and former lover than as a wife?" I leaned over and tucked a red curl behind her ear.

"I don't know," she mumbled, as she hid her face with her hands.

"It's not just a job, it's who I am. I can't change who I am, Gelly."

"I know. That's what Tante Clothilde told me." She took a steadying breath as Stella dropped off our meals, and we ate in silence.

"I think I need a break. I need to think. Losing Alex nearly did me in, Etienne. It took a lot to recover to get back to me. These scars, as much as I hate them, they sometimes feel so right. They show the world all the broken pieces inside me, like tattoos that God gave me, so I don't forget."

"You don't have to forget, Gelly. You have to forgive yourself, and you have to live. Maybe not with me. I get it. My life, my job, they're dangerous. But that is what I do—"

"—You don't think I know that? Theo was like that, a protector. Beau is like that. It's something I admire about you … but I don't know if I can live through all the constant fear. In here." She covered her heart with a balled-up fist. "I need to think, to process. Can you just give me that time?"

"I can, but don't take too long." My work phone rang, interrupting us again. "Deputy Benoit," I paused, "I'm on my way." I looked at Gelly, "I have to go. Are you going back home?"

"First there, but then to the studio. I have to dance to think." She got up and grabbed her purse.

I nodded, threw down a twenty for breakfast, and then kissed her tenderly. "Don't think for too long."

We both walked our separate ways to our cars. En route to mine, I called back the dispatcher Brenda. "What did you need me to listen to?"

"Deputy Benoit, a Miss Dupuy, is on the line. She says your fiancée, Angelle, is in trouble."

In the background, I heard Caroline's voice. "In danger! I mean it."

"Caroline? This is Etienne, tell me." I ran back to catch Gelly, but her car was already gone.

"I'm an idiot, Etienne." Her breath hitched. "I met a guy at the Cowboys. I was bitching about you and how you were engaged to Angelle. He seemed like he was a good listener. Plus, he was big and gorgeous. Anyway, I drank too much and took him home." Then her sobbing stopped her explanation.

Inhaling, I asked, as patiently as I could, "Caroline, what does this have to do with Angelle?"

Her words rushed out. "After we, you know ... well, he beat the shit out of me and then he stole my car. I think he's after Angelle." More sobs. I drove my patrol car towards the Babineaux Farm.

I gentled my voice. "So, he has your car, and you think he's after Angelle? What's the make and model of your car?" Caroline told the dispatcher the make and model.

"One more thing, Etienne. He asked a lot of questions about her. He especially wanted to know where she worked."

I stopped in the middle of the road, switched on my lights, and headed to *Le Carré* and Gelly's studio.

"I'm sorry, Etienne," she sobbed again.

"I need to go, Caroline. Thank you for calling this in. Brenda, can you get her information and send some EMTs to her house? Also, we will need some backup at the Babineaux farm and Angelle's studio, *Dance avec moi*, in *Le Carré*."

"Will do, Deputy."

"I'm so sorry, Etienne," I heard Caroline repeat.

"Gotta go. Thank you, Caroline." I was speeding as fast as my patrol car could go at this point. En route, I did a group speaker call with the Krewe.

"Anyone have eyes on Gelly? I have credible information that Ray is after her."

"She left her house a while ago. I think she just zipped in for her dance bag," Beau said.

"Armand, she said she was going to her studio. Do you have eyes on her?"

"I've been here for a while. I did see Gelly get here, but then Renee came by and asked me what I was doing. He could have snuck in during that time," Armand admitted.

"I'm heading to the studio to check on her now," I told them.

"I'll meet you there," Beau said.

"No, he might also target her house. Stay put. We got this."

"I'm sorry guys," Marc interjected, "Sofia got sick, I'm dropping her at grandma's, and I'm on my way."

"Marc, go to the farm. If we missed Gelly leaving the studio, the danger might be there," I reiterated.

"I'll head there then. That's much closer."

"Armand, go around back. Gelly has a key under the doormat in the back—," I told him.

"—That is the worst place to put one," Armand interrupted.

"I know, but Ray probably went in that way, and thus he probably used the key. See if the back door is opened. We are coming in loud with sirens. I need you to be stealthy while I and my backup distract Ray."

"Roger that."

"Armand, you're carrying, right?" Etienne asked.

"As if you have to ask. Just get your ass over here."

19

Dangerous Dance

Angelle

I had to think, and the only way I could think was if I danced.
I entered my studio and put on my thinking playlist. First up
was *Waltzing's for Dreamers* by Richard Thompson, to which
I danced a slowed down version of Balanchine's *Waltz of the
Flowers* dance scene. I continued by dancing the *Dying Swan* by
Tchaikovsky as the music switched over to Linda Thompson's
version of *Walking on the Wire*. The dance stopped a few
moments before the music, so I just improvised as I thought.

When the music ended, I knew I wasn't just 'fallin' as the
song discussed. I had already fallen. I was in love with Etienne,
just like I admitted when he was unconscious. No matter what
happened to him, I would feel it. There was no way to avoid it.
So, my choice was to ignore my emotions, avoid love, and get
hurt anyway. Or do what I was best at, feel my emotions deeply.
I smiled and took down my hair, shaking it out; just because I
loved Etienne didn't mean I had to admit it to him. I needed
more time. Then I heard the clapping.

A man I didn't recognize was standing in my studio.

"Who are you?"

"Aw, sweetheart, you don't remember me?" I cocked my head to the side and then it hit me. The fire. This was the man who worked with Shell's ex. The *fils d'putain* who tried to smoke us out. He fired into the camp when I checked for an escape route out the back window. He was huge. I remembered Tanner calling him Ultron Ray.

"Ah, I see you remember now. I'm the one that put those pretty scars on you, killed your husband, too."

My hand instinctually went to my face. Traitorous hand. "Doug killed my husband." *Keep calm, Gelly. Think!*

"Doug was a moron and a scared one at that. I gave him a choice: Get rid of your hubby, or I would get rid of him. I got stuck with him as a partner. Assigned, if you would." Ray took a step closer, and I backed up.

"Assigned by whom?"

"Well, look at you with your fancy language. I heard from Caroline that you even think you can speak French. Well, Miss, since you won't be telling anyone anything, I'll let you know that Bill Breaux needs the Hebert brats out of the picture. That just worked out since Doug needed that stupid bitch of an ex-wife gone as well."

"The school wasn't even his inheritance." *Exits, exits, where are the damn exits?* Ray blocked the rear exit, and I didn't think I could get to the front one before he caught me.

Ray stalked towards me. He smiled when I flinched at each step. "Yeah, well, the boss man didn't know that. What he did know is that he could get the school land and the Heberts' money simply by burning one camp."

I flushed, my nostrils flaring. "Well, he didn't get either, did he?!"

"Not yet," Ray taunted. *What a tchu!*

"Hurting me won't get you the land or the Heberts' money." *Weapon, I need a weapon. Malheureusement,* dance leotards did not come equipped with weapons. I scanned the room.

"Maybe not. You don't have to know the plan. Just know that you're payback. Payback for that stupid deputy that winged me. I'm going to play with his toy and then leave you as a message." I was almost within arm's reach of him, with my back against the wall. *Talk, just keep him talking. Etienne, now is the time for telepathy.* "And how will that help you get the Heberts?"

"Because you, my ugly little creature, are just a distraction. A fragile, wonderfully breakable distraction. While Deputy Benoit was convalescing in your delicate little arms, I was making plans."

"What plans?" I slid against the wall towards the front of the room, but he just made up the distance.

"Keep him talking. Is that what you want to do? Okay, I'll tell you, bitch, because you'll not survive to tell a soul. I had to hole up in a pay-as-you-go, shitty motel, and use all my money. Fucking Breaux nearly washed his hands of me. Stupid Val died swearing she knew nothing, begging me not to hurt her kids, but I don't give up, do I, dearie? Ray Jones will always survive. This time I found a lush trolling for college boys."

"This story is boring, Ray." I slid closer to the front window. Pretending to be looking out. They might not be able to save me, but maybe they could shoot Ray through the window.

"Would you like me to relieve you of your boredom?" His smirk snatched my breath.

"So, you met a lush." *Running out of time. Keep him talking.* I tried to calm my heart rate. My limbs were trembling.

"After a drink or three, the blond bimbo told me that I know how to treat a woman unlike a certain deputy, who now was engaged to some scarred tramp. She wished that fire had finished you off. Can you imagine my surprise? She said that, apparently, the deputy likes delicate little flowers with big insurance checks. And how you, my scarred beastie, bankrolled your own dance school. Of course, I had to know more. After all, this was the bastard that shot me."

"Of course," I agreed, because what else does one say to a homicidal narcissist?

"That must have been some check, my little beastie," He looked around the studio. "Who knew accountants were worth so much? So, then I just pretended to know where the school was. She corrected me and pointed me straight to you. Of course, the lush did complain about the name of the school. Something about you being a pretentious bitch that spoke a countrified French that she couldn't understand."

Ahh … Cruella, the idiot. "So, then you just rushed on over here?"

"Well, first I made use of what was offered to me. Then I made sure she wouldn't be talking and borrowed her car to come visit you." He moved toward me.

I said a quick prayer for Cruella. If this was the end, I didn't want that on my conscience. *Questions, Gelly, ask another question.* My voice wobbled. "And your plan is what? To kill me? Why?"

Ray heard the terror, and his mouth canted in glee. "My plan is to use you as leverage, or just use you. As long as I get something out of it."

I shivered, gagged, and darted to the other side of the room, but Ray cornered me. He grabbed me. As I struggled, he grabbed my hair, pulling my head back to reveal my scars.

He kissed my neck. I whimpered. "These scars make me smile, knowing that you always think of me when you look at them. Indelibly imprinted on you."

I shook my head. *Get a grip, Gelly. If this is the end, you will not go down whimpering.* I stared him dead in the eye. "When I look at my scars, I don't think of the idiot who set the fire—the hired help. I think of the children that I rescued. I gave a piece of myself to keep them safe."

"Well, you will be giving a bit more than that this time." Ray reached over and traced the scar with a gun that he pulled from behind him. Sirens sounded outside and footsteps ran towards the studio. "I would have loved to have time to play with you, but apparently we're out of time."

"You are out of time," Etienne said from behind him. My body relaxed when I heard his voice.

"Deputy, nice of you to arrive, but if you don't put down your weapon, this scarred little creature will be dead." Ray positioned me between himself, Etienne, and the front door. Ensuring that there was no clear shot of him except through me. "So, what you're going to do is clear a path for me and your ugly little creature to leave."

I winced as he grabbed me by my hair. "It's a distraction, Etienne. They're after the Littles."

"Do you trust me, Gelly?" Etienne asked, and I nodded.

Ray sneered, "You'll be too late, and then you won't save the brats or your little creature here."

Etienne placed his gun on the floor and raised his hands.

"And I heard you were the bright one," Ray gloated, as he aimed at Etienne.

"No!" I said, as Ray flung me away so he could steady the gun with two hands. Before he could pull the trigger, a shot came from the back of the studio and Ray went down.

Etienne ran to me, "Are you okay, Gelly?" His hands started searching for wounds.

"I'm fine, you idiot. You put down your gun. You're a moron. Why do I love such a *couillon*? The Littles! What about them? That's who they're after."

"Marc and Beau are both there and more backup as well." He looked toward a deputy at the door, who nodded.

"Hey Trouble, they headed there as soon as one of the other deputies overheard Ray." Armand said, emerging from the shadows.

"Shots fired at the Babineaux Farm," came over his vest radio.

"On my way," Etienne said and looked at Armand. "Guard her."

Armand nodded, but I got up and followed Etienne out. "That's my home, and my family. I'm going with you."

"You're no fragile flower." Etienne grinned at me, knowing he couldn't stop me. I jumped in as he opened the back door of his cruiser for me, after which he and Armand jumped in the front seats.

"Steel Magnolia, baby," I agreed.

"You will stay in the car until I give the all clear."

"As you wish," I told him docilely.

"Why does that not sound like a yes?" Etienne asked Armand.

"Because it wasn't," he responded.

By the time we made it to the Babineaux farm, there were already police, fire trucks, and ambulances at the property.

Etienne and Armand were getting out when I said, "Bill Breaux, that's who is behind all this. Ray told me because he thought I'd be dead and couldn't tell anyone."

"You got that name, Brenda?" Etienne spoke into his radio vest.

"Sure thing, Deputy Benoit. I'll talk to the station about writing up the paperwork for a warrant."

I tried to open my door.

"Patience, Gelly. I need to know it's safe," he said, locking his car, drowning out my angry words. But I'm certain he caught the insults 'overbearing and duplicitous' as he remarked, "Her vocabulary gets fancy when she's mad. Something I'll have to keep in mind when we get married."

"Beau is going to kill you."

Etienne shrugged. "He'll maim me at the most." Then he turned to Armand and said as they walked away, "Let's see what kind of FUBAR we have here." I tried the door again. That *fils d'putain* locked me in!

20

Clean Up

Etienne

Armand and I first checked on Shell and the Littles. The Littles were on the porch with their parents, curious as to what was going on. No doubt the 'rents had kept them from seeing the worst of it.

"Where's Marc?" I asked.

Beau pointed across the field to the EMT truck. "Glancing wound, possible concussion."

We turned to check on him when Val escaped the porch and ran to me. "*Parrain!*"

As Armand made his way to the EMT truck, I turned and grabbed up Val in a big hug. She smelled like candy and shampoo. *The happy child smells.* "Hey there Val. You doing okay?"

"The tangos tried to get us, but Mr. Marc and Dad ... M. [*Monsieur*] Beau fought them off." I smirked at Val and glanced at Beau, who was standing taller now, since he heard Val's near slip.

"The tangos, huh?"

"Well, they might have been mercs. That's what Dad ... M. Beau said."

"Tangos are what we call bad guys, but mercs just means military people hired privately for a job. They're not all bad." As I spoke, I walked her back up to the porch and handed her to Beau, who squeezed her tightly for good measure.

"These ones were," she whispered into Beau's neck and put her head on his shoulder.

"Indeed, they were. I need to check on things out there. You have everything in hand over here, *ma belle*?" She smiled at the endearment and leaned over for another hug. I picked her back up, gave her a big hug, and when she let go, I set her down on the porch.

"I'm on it, *parrain*. I'm fixin' hot chocolate and reading to the Littles just like Mam ... *Madame* Michelle taught me to."

"You're a good sister and a great goddaughter. Now, you work on getting the Littles calm, and I will check on Mr. Marc. Deal?"

"Deal." She blew me a kiss and added, "I love you."

"I love you, too, and I promise to keep you safe."

"Of course you will," she said, as she herded her brothers and sister into the house. "Otherwise, Daddy will kick your *tchu*."

When I turned, both Beau's and Shell's eyes were glossy with tears.

"You're going to punish her for her language, *Daddy*?" I emphasized the last word.

"Not this time, no," Beau said, swallowing and wiping his eyes.

When Val went in the house, I nodded to him. "This is all about them. We need a plan to keep them safer."

Beau reached for Shell, who had stiffened at that statement. "Let's hang tonight and discuss it."

"I'll let the Krewe know. I'm gonna go check on Marc," she said.

"See you soon," he nodded.

Marc shrugged off the EMT, who was trying to check his eyes. "I'm fine."

"You're stubborn, not the same thing." She tried to shine a flashlight into Marc's eyes again. He turned away again.

I laughed as I walked up, and Armand smiled. "You're not by any chance related to my nanny, Clothilde Benoit, are you?" I asked the EMT.

"No, but Ms. Clothilde and I are on the same committees at St. Francis. I love her. I want to be her when I grow up," she said.

I grinned. "You're well on your way. My nanny would be proud."

"Do we know you from somewhere?" Armand added.

"Do you read? I'm also a librarian at the public library in Breaux Bridge. Kayleigh Breaux."

"Nice to meet you Kayleigh, now can I please go? I need to pick up my daughter." Marc rose from his seat in the back of the ambulance.

Kayleigh pushed him back to a seated position. "No. Absolutely not."

"What do you mean 'no'? I need to pick her up!" Marc scowled up at her as she made a third attempt to shine a flashlight into his eyes. Again, he turned away.

"If you have a concussion, which I can't tell since you're too stubborn to let me check, then you should not drive your daughter anywhere. You will put her life in danger."

"I don't have a concussion," Marc insisted.

"Really? So, you can tell if your own eyes are dilating or not?"

"We got this," Armand said, flashing his super powerful flashlight in Marc's eyes, while I held his head still.

Marc said, "Dammit, Armand!"

The EMT peered into his eyes and noted their response. "Not dilating. You, sir, have a concussion."

"I have to get Sofia. My mom has an afternoon shift today,and she can't watch her now." Marc tried getting up again. This time, I shoved him down.

"Give me your keys," Armand told him. "I'll go and get her." Marc handed his keys over, and Armand ran to his SUV.

"And I will get going. My shift ended an hour ago. No driving. Concussions can affect depth perception, which you need to be safe on the road. Also, if you experience nausea, dizziness, or vomiting, go to the hospital," the EMT warned. With that, she turned and walked away.

"Thanks?" Marc said, getting up to watch her retreating form as she walked to the front of her vehicle. When he turned, I was there waiting.

"Tell me what happened." We walked away from the houses as all the emergency vehicles left the property.

"Four tangos, from what we could see. I took out two and grappled with a third. Shell, being a true mama bear, took out another. The one that had scaled the wall and was attempting to enter through a window in the house."

"Beau's been taking her to the range to practice?"

"Yep. Then the one I grappled with escaped. I chased him across the field and knocked him into the pond."

"There's one to interrogate?"

"Yep, but like I said, they looked like mercs. Chances are we won't get much from him."

"Fan out. Let's see if they left anything behind. Wait, a second." I took out my phone and whispered into it. Marc smiled when he heard Beau laughing through the phone.

"What's up?"

"I left Gelly locked in the back of my car. I'm getting Beau to come and get my keys so he can let her out."

Marc shook his head. "You are *for sure* not doing this courting thing right."

"I'm new to it. Bound to make mistakes," I said, shrugging my shoulders.

Armand shook his head. "She's going to be pissed."

"Which is why I'm getting Beau to let her out. I'll head back once she cools off."

"Idiot," Marc whispered and then fanned to the east to scan for clues.

We found both an abandoned van and skid marks from a vehicle that had left the scene in a hurry.

"Expect more," Marc said under his breath.

"Yep, we need to protect the Littles. This is about them."

"How do you know?"

"Ray told Gelly, before we got there," I explained.

Beau walked across the field to greet us. I tossed him my keys, and he tossed them back. "Gibb's Rule #45: Clean up your own mess."

"Crap. I was hoping fraternal love would calm her down."

"Word to the wise from an old married man. Do *not* tell her to calm down. Just don't."

I ran across the field to my vehicle. Gelly was laying back on the seat kicking at the window.

"Will you stop that? You're going to hurt yourself." I rushed over, unlocked, and then opened the door. As I let her out of the car, Gelly glared at me and punched me on the arm.

"Ow!" She packed a wallop. Then she grabbed me and kissed me deeply, and then punched me on the arm again. "Ow! Sorry *mon amour*. I have to keep you safe." I rubbed my sore shoulder.

"I'm not a doll to be put up. Also, you could have just walked me over to the house to be with Shell." She pointed to the porch in question.

I shook my head. "Had to keep you out of the kill zone."

"Me loving you is going to drive me crazy, won't it?"

I grinned and singsonged, "You lub me. You want to marry me."

"*Couillon!*" She stomped over to Beau and Shell's house, with me following behind her, grinning. When she got there, she hugged Shell, and then went inside to hug the Littles.

Shell followed her inside. After she shooed the Littles to bed, promising to head up soon to read to them, she said, "C'mon, I think we need some tea after this ordeal." She grabbed Gelly's arm and pulled her into the kitchen. I followed because I was thirsty too.

"Long Island for me, please." Shell chuckled and nodded at Gelly's drink order.

"You've earned it!" She started mixing her a drink as Gelly sat at the kitchen table watching. With her elbow on the table and her chin in her hand, she sighed heavily.

"Maybe make it a double, will ya?" Shell nodded, added a shot, and put Gelly's drink in front of her. Then she poured me some sweet tea.

A few minutes later, Beau bounded in from the porch and made a beeline to the kitchen. "Gelly, I need to know exactly what Ray, the bastard, told you."

"Ray!" Shell tensed and crossed the kitchen to lock the side door. "Is he around?"

Gelly patted Shell's back. "He's gone. Thanks to Armand and this moron that I love making a target of himself."

Gelly pointed at me, and I preened. "She loves me." Gelly rolled her eyes, and Shell pressed her lips together to keep from smiling. Then I reached over and grabbed Gelly, hugging her to me. Gelly leaned in for a moment, sighed, and then pushed me away.

"I do love you, but I'm in a mood to maim you right now, so back off."

Nodding my head and making slow movements, like a lion tamer, I nodded. "Not a problem; I can do that. Now spill. What all did Ray say?"

"I'm not repeating myself, and the rest of your Krewe will absolutely ask. Let's just gather everyone together, and then I'll tell you anything you need." I smiled and lifted my eyebrows hopefully. "However," Gelly continued, "If you ask me tonight to marry, move in, or date you for real, I will decline." She pointed at me. "Eye on the ball, Deputy Benoit. You have a bad guy to catch."

I smiled, winked at Shell, who giggled, and I said, "Understood. I'll get the gang together."

"The gang's all here!" Marc called from the door.

"Except Armand," Beau added. Then we heard Marc's SUV drive up. "Never mind, I spoke too soon."

Outside, Armand parked, walked around the car, and then lifted a giggling girl fireman style to the porch.

"Somebody call for a princess?" he asked, as Bailey Marie ran in from her room.

"Mama, can Sofia play in my room?" Tears welled up in Shell's eyes as she nodded and both girls ran from the room.

"You know she's going to start to realize that she just needs to call you Mama to get her way," Beau whispered to her.

"Big talk from a guy who recently cried because Val called you Daddy."

"You're both suckers, adorable suckers." Gelly told them.

Then Sofia came back. "Mr. Armand? Mawmaw Richard always says girls are queens and not princesses. We don't need to be rescued. I'm a queen."

"So noted, Queen Sofia." I genuflected and Sofia skipped out of the room, giggling as her dark black hair in long pigtails trailed behind her.

Armand stared pointedly at Marc, who shrugged. "What? My mom is a big feminist."

"She'll grow up to be a strong woman," Gelly said. "Although, I will say that I do thank you both for the rescue this evening."

"Of course, Gelly," Armand said. "You are still a queen in my book." Gelly hugged him.

"Hey!" I grumbled.

"Hey, yourself. Armand is family," Gelly said.

"Well, family, let's get some libations and talk because it looks like Gelly has some splainin' to do," Shell said. Herding everyone into the living room, she passed out shots and beers to everyone except Gelly, to whom she handed a second tall glass of Long Island Iced Tea.

"Not fair," Armand said.

"She might get parched, and this is what she ordered. Ignore him, Gelly, and just tell us what that *fils d'putain* Ray told you," Shell told her.

Gelly took a giant swig of the tea, took a deep breath, then told us about the Littles, inheritances, and how the fire wasn't Doug's idea. She told us it was the plan of a Mr. William Breaux, whose main goal was to kill the Littles.

"He wanted the land the school was on as well, so for him it was a win/win."

We heard giggling from the kids' rooms.

"I'm ... uh ... Just going to go and check on them," Shell said.

A car came screeching to a halt outside the door. Beau sprinted upstairs, Marc ran to the back door in the kitchen, and Armand peered out the window while I shoved Gelly behind me.

Armand called out, "Stand down. It's just Renee. Jeez Louise, what's she doing here?!" He griped as he slammed out the door. Once outside, Renee and Armand began to argue.

"What the hell are you doing here? You drove out here alone?"

"There were police at the studio. They said someone attacked my cousin. Since no one called me, I went to the hospital. When she wasn't there, I came here."

"Ok, folks, let's not frighten the Littles. They have been through enough," Gelly said calmly and opened her arms to hug Renee. Armand saw the looming tears then and grimaced, no doubt feeling like an ogre.

"Sorry, Renny," he said. Renee nodded and clung to Gelly as she entered the house.

"Everyone is safe, Renee." She hugged her close. "Armand, since you are outside already, why not get the fire pit started? You and the boys can discuss ... things ... while we talk to Renee." He nodded, walked over to the fire pit, and started loading in wood.

21

Porch Sitting

Angelle

As I set up the porch with steaming hot chocolate and a selection of liquors, Etienne prepared a cooler filled with LA 31 Bayou Teche Brewery beers. He then joined the rest of the Krewe at the fire pit.

Shell and I assured the Littles that everything was alright and that their aunt Renee had just come to visit.

Val suggested, "She can do a sleepover with me, if she wants, since Sofia is with Bailey Marie."

"I will let her know, sweetheart. For now, just rest for nap time." Shell kissed her forehead.

"I love you, Mama."

"I love you, too, Val. You sleep well."

"I'm glad you're here, Nanny. Love you."

I kissed her on the forehead and said, "Love you, too, Val."

As Shell and I closed the door, I saw a faint light come on under the door. Reading by flashlight, Val really was a doppelgänger of her adopted mother. Another great German word. Then we went to the front porch to have some girl-talk time and solve world problems.

On the porch, I made my own spiked hot chocolate with a shot of Kahlua, Baileys, Frangelico, and some Jameson whiskey. My third drink of the day.

"Any hot chocolate in there?" Renee teased.

"Not much. It has been a day." I sat on the porch swing and chortled as Renee fixed herself an even more spiked hot chocolate than mine. Then she plopped down next to me.

"So, I heard ... from the cop that was guarding your studio—"

"—Is there a lot of damage?" I sipped and then grimaced at the rush of alcohol. "I don't remember. It's all a blur."

"Not that I could see." Renee leaned against me as she took another sip and nodded. We swung on the porch swing as we watched the men at the fire pit.

"They sure are pretty," Renee stated, and I put my head against her shoulder and tittered.

"That they are." But my eyes focused on one particular man. Then I sighed. "Lessons start in a couple of days. I hope this won't scare people away."

Shell came through the front door. "Meauxville people?! Please! They'll all show up, if for nothing else than to get the scoop," Shell said, and settled in a rocking chair. She had herbal tea in her cup and gazed wistfully at my hot chocolate.

"And to see if they can help. Remember how many came to help clear away the debris from the burned camp?" Renee added and handed her cup to Shell, who shook her head.

Shell turned to me. "Now, catch me up."

"So, Ray, before he was taken care of, told me that there is a kingpin, William Breaux, pulling the strings. The attack on me was a distraction so they could get the Littles. Ray mentioned some kind of inheritance." As I spoke, I drew up my knees and put my arms around them, taking comfort in the position. Shell put her hand on my shoulder, but at the mention of the Littles, all movement stopped.

Renee broke the silence. "Why would anyone want them dead? They were just poor orphans."

"Excuse me?!" Shell scowled.

"You know I don't mean it like that, Shell. I mean, they're not rich, they don't have property. There's no inheritance. What is the motivation for Breaux, who appears to be a bigwig, to risk everything and attack them?"

"You're right," I nodded. "It doesn't make sense."

"Clearly there's something that we don't know," Shell said, sipping her herbal tea, pondering, while rocking on her chair. "I'll ask the Littles to try to think of any family they might have."

"What we really need," Renee said, "is someone to search the parish records, including birth and death certificate."

Shell and Renee's eyes met, and each smirked, and then they nodded.

"What? Y'all have an idea? If so, you need to share."

"Librarian," Renee said, and Shell nodded. "We need a librarian, and I know just the one. She even knows some of what's going on. I'll text her now. Kayleigh will come right over." Renee pulled out her phone, texted, read a text, laughed, and texted again.

"She is en route, but she said something about avoiding stubborn idiots. She's a hoot."

"In the interim, let's talk logistics." Shell rubbed her hands together in anticipation. "Now that you have finally admitted you love Etienne."

"What logistics? I'm just getting my dream school started, and he's moving, God knows where, once he gets into the FBI. We're doomed." I put my face in my hands.

"Well, as long as you are starting with a positive, optimistic attitude, what can go wrong?" Shell patted me on the shoulder. "Listen." She nudged me with her finger. "You can solve anything with logistics."

"C'mon Gelly, we're educators, we're logistic experts. List the problems, and we will solve them." My head came up at Renee's statement.

"The first problem is where to live. I love it here." I motioned toward the entire property.

"That is not a problem. This will always be your home and you own part of the land. Next problem." Shell made a checking motion with her finger, took another sip of tea and grimaced again.

"You need to find some other tea," I told her.

"It's good for me and Jr. here." She patted her stomach as she rocked on the rocking chair. "So, I'll stick with the yucky tea. Next problem."

"Well, we still haven't solved the 'where will we live?' problem."

Renee took a sip of her spiked cocoa and snorted, "That's easy. Gelly, you live in a tiny home and tiny homes move. So, you'll find a lot wherever he lands, and you'll live there." Then she also made the checking motion. I sighed.

"That might work, although Etienne barely fits in my home. However, that brings me to the biggest hurdle. My school is my dream. Alex and I worked hard to make it come to fruition. I love Etienne, but do I have to give up my dream for love?"

"No!" Shell and Renee yelled in unison.

"Everything okay over there?" Beau called from the fire pit. Shell smiled. Her man was always there for her.

"Everything's fine, sweetheart; we're just chatting about female things."

He held up his hands as if to stop her. "Nuff said. Let me know if you need anything."

"Will do." Shell blew a kiss to him.

"As we were saying," Renee continued, "if you give up on your dream, then you will end up regretting that decision and blaming Etienne. Plus, he would never ask you to do that, right?"

I shook my head. "Never, but the problem remains. The FBI doesn't have an office in Meauxville. He's going to be assigned somewhere far away."

Renee took another swig of her spiked cocoa. "So, then you need to do what thousands of business owners do, and that is to figure out a way to run your business remotely."

I interrupted Renee's virtual checkmark. "—But I *want* to be there for the recitals and rehearsals and graduations," I whined.

"So, be there for those events and leave the day-to-day minutia to someone else." Renee finished her check mark.

"Hmm," I thought for a bit while Shell and Renee sipped and watched me.

"I could get instructors who have graduated from nearby schools to teach classes. I would need to hire a manager."

"Easy enough," Renee said and leaned back to finish off her cocoa. "I think I've earned a second cup."

"I need paper and a pen. You know, my friend Sarah might be able to help. She's student-teaching now, but I bet she could run it as a part-time job. She's super organized." I smiled at the idea of working with my bestie.

Shell turned her head at that. "Student teaching? In elementary? Does she speak French?" Renee and I laughed. Shell was constantly looking for local French Immersion teachers.

"She only knows the bad words," I said.

"If she knows the bad words, she can learn the good ones. Give me her contact information. If she works at Académie School, she'll only be two blocks from the studio. So, if there's an emergency at the studio, I can let her go and check on it."

"Get me that pen and paper for my plan, and I'll zap you her contact information."

"Deal!" Shell turned to go into the house to get them, when a car drove up and honked.

"That must be Kayleigh," Renee said, and then the shouting started.

22

Campfire

Etienne

While the ladies were solving all the logistical problems, we men were discussing Mr. Breaux and how to find out what was really going on with the Littles. We drank our beer and stared into the fire pit on our Adirondack patio chairs. As we sipped, we discussed the case.

"Any updates on the SUV plate?" Marc asked Etienne.

"Stolen about a week ago *en ville*," I said absently. Then I mused, "I feel like Chretien Point is important. Ray went there several times. I feel like that means something. He brought Valerie, the Littles' mom, there. He killed her there. Then he went back again when he attacked me. He didn't go there to attack me; he was seen there doing something when we responded to the BOLO."

"It might have something to do with this." Marc held up the key I had found before Ray shot me.

Armand took the key to look at it. "The whole plantation thing is weird. What would an old run-down plantation have to do with the Littles? But this," Armand held up the key, "looks like a safe deposit box key."

"Lots of questions, and I'm sure we'll find answers. For now," Beau looked over to the porch. "I need ... we need to make sure the Littles and those around them are safe." There were nods all around. "I can watch over them at school." He looked at me. "Even Gelly when she's teaching there."

"I can beef up all the security systems," Marc volunteered. Beau nodded, and Marc got on his phone to make arrangements.

Armand crossed his arms over his chest. "I'm on leave until after Christmas. I can keep an eye on everyone while y'all are at work. I'll just make a circuit between the Babineaux compound, *Le Carré*, and the school."

We heard a loud "No!" from the porch.

"Everything okay over there?" Beau called, standing up to look over. Shell smiled, and he relaxed.

"Everything's fine sweetheart, we are just chatting about female things."

He held up his hands as if to stop her. "Nuff said, let me know if you need anything." He sat back down and we continued to contemplate the fire quietly.

A few minutes later, a car screeched into the drive and honked. We were immediately up and moving toward the car. Marc got to the driver's side quickly.

"What are you doing here?" He knocked on the driver's side window. It was the snarky blond miniature EMT.

The little blond rolled down her window because Marc was blocking the door. "Excuse me, I was invited. What are you doing here? Shouldn't you be in bed sleeping with someone waking you up every hour?"

"These are my friends. We're trying to figure out what's going on. I don't even know why I'm telling you."

"I'm here for the same reason."

"It's okay, Marc. We called Kayleigh to come over," Renee yelled out to him.

"Why?" Marc stepped back to let Kayleigh open the door.

"Because if you want to figure something out, then you need a librarian. It's what we do." Kayleigh pushed open the door and made her way to the porch. Halfway there, she stopped and looked at the fire pit and the beer bottles next to the chairs. Then she turned to Marc. With her hands on her hips, she glared at Marc. "Have you been drinking?!"

Marc shrugged his shoulders. "What? I just had a beer."

"Who's the idiot that gave the man with a concussion a beer?" Kayleigh yelled. "You can't drink alcohol if you have a concussion." We all took a step back. Kayleigh huffed, "*Espèce d'idiots*," under her breath, and stomped to the porch.

Shell greeted her with a cup of cocoa. "Spiked," she told her. Kayleigh smiled and took a gulp. Coughing at the amount of alcohol. Shell sat back down and called over to us. "Beau, *cheri*, get Marc a nice cold coke."

Beau walked over, poured Marc's beer onto the fire, and asked, "What'll it be?"

Marc shook his head. "I should be able to decide if I drink a beer or not."

Beau nodded his head. "True, true, but you're my guest and also Tanner's *parrain*, so when my wife says you don't drink, to protect you, then, my friend, you don't drink. What'll it be?"

"Sprite," Marc said, staring daggers at Kayleigh.

"I'll get it and some more chairs. Now that the expert is here, you boys will want to hear what she has to say. C'mon up!" With that, Renee disappeared into the house.

Armand went up the stairs as well, calling to Renee. "I'll get the chairs; you get the Sprite."

Once everyone got situated on the porch, they re-introduced us to Kayleigh and briefly outlined for her everything that had happened.

"Wow, y'all have been busy." She took a deep drink from her cocoa. "This is delicious," she told Renee. "Okay, here are our angles as I see them." She pulled out a notebook from the back pocket of her jeans and started making a list. "One, we need to do a deep dive on the Hebert's line. We have a whole genealogy section at the library, so I can do that. Was Hebert their mama's maiden name?"

"Hebert was her maiden name. That is also the only name she has on the Little's birth certificates. There is no father mentioned," Beau told her.

Kayleigh noted that down and then tapped her finger on her cheek, probably thinking. "No father at all? Because we need a deep dive into that name as well."

Shell shook her head. "I've already asked them about that. They have no idea who their father is. Ms. Hebert was the only one to raise them. We don't even know about her family. All the Heberts I've asked have no idea which branch of the family tree Valerie came from."

Kayleigh tapped on her cheek again. "No problem, no problem. Let's try the property angle. You said that events seem to be revolving around Chretien Point? Then we need to gather information about the property. Who owns it now? Who owned it in the past? That's in city, parish, and state records." She looked at me in my deputy's uniform.

"I can look into all that easily enough," I nodded to her.

"Finally, we need to look into Bill Breaux. It's a fairly common name. I even have an uncle named Bill Breaux. Since you mentioned gambling and a casino, let's check on any William/Bill Breaux with links to a casino property or license. Once we're sure who the players are, I can do a genealogy search. Deputy—"

"—Etienne," I corrected.

"Etienne, can you look into legally filed paperwork about the school land and Chretien point? Also, see if any of the Louisiana casinos have a partner, silent or otherwise, named Bill Breaux. If we can find Mr. Breaux, then we need someone to look into his social presence. Track articles about him, friend him using a junk account online, just see what he's doing."

"I can do that," Gelly said. Beau and I jumped up and objected almost immediately.

"I don't want you on his radar!" I said as I eased beside her and put my hands on her shoulders.

"Too late. He already sent someone to burn me and then kill me. What more could he do?" She took a deep swig of her cocoa.

"We'll talk about this tonight, when we're alone," I told her and took her cup. Then I sniffed it. "Is this spiked cocoa?" Gelly swayed when she got up.

"It is. I had a rough day, so I got rewarded with libations." I frowned at Shell.

"What? We're grown women. We can drink if we want to. Well, I can't, but Gelly can."

I steadied Gelly as she giggled, trying to get off the porch. "We'll talk about this tomorrow."

Gelly leaned over the back of the porch swing and kissed me. "No, no, we won't, but you can try to change my mind." She comically raised her eyebrows.

Beau put his hands over his ears. "Make it stop!" Gelly chuckled.

"I guess that means the party's over," Kayleigh announced. She pulled out her car keys and got up to leave. She, too, swayed and nearly toppled over.

Marc had to prop her up. "Wow, that was one strong cocoa."

"I'll drive her home," Marc said, taking her keys.

Kayleigh grabbed them back and scolded, slurring some because the liquor just hit her. "Did you listen to nofing I told you? You have a con con concussion. You should not be driving and should not be alone!"

"We have a guest bedroom," Beau offered. "At least that's what it is right now." He looked over at Shell, and she blushed.

"Aw, y'all are so cute," Kayleigh said. "But I'm not sharing a bed with this guy. I barely know him." The ladies found that vastly amusing.

Marc shook his head. "No! I'll take the couch and you can sleep in the guest bedroom."

"Oh," Kayleigh said. *Did she sound disappointed? Interesting development.*

As Marc got up to help her up and into the house, the porch door swung open and Sofia and Bailey Marie ran out. "Miss Kayleigh! Miss Kayleigh!" Bailey Marie and Sofia were out the door and hugging her. Marc was looking pissed.

"Are we doing story time here tomorrow?" Sofia asked her.

"Queen Sofia and Queen Bailey Marie, your wishes are my command, but let me sleep late, okay?" she said as Marc opened the porch door for her.

They giggled, hugged her, and said, "*'Twas brillig, and the slithy toves. Did gyre and gimble in the wabe,*" to which Kayleigh responded, "*All mimsy were the borogoves, and the mome raths outgrabe.*" They giggled again, noticing Marc's frown of consternation.

Sofia told him, "That's from *Alice in Wonderland*. It was from the 'Jabberwocky' poem. Ms. Kayleigh always starts story time with that poem."

"Well, aren't you two literary," Marc said and leaned down to grab them up to carry them to bed.

I stayed him with my hand. "Nope. Concussion, remember. I've got them. You just show Ms. Kayleigh the guest room, and we will follow." I swooped both girls up, one in each arm as they chortled. "Stay here," I told Gelly. She stuck her tongue out at me, setting off another round of giggles.

"Fine," she said and went to sit down on the porch steps.

"What's litter berry?" Bailey Marie asked as we made our way to her room.

"It means you like books," I told her as I opened the door to her room.

"We do!" they both said simultaneously. I smiled, swung them around, and plopped them both down on Bailey-Marie's bed.

"I'm glad to hear it," Marc said from behind me, and then he tucked both girls in.

"Night Daddy! Night M. Etienne." Sofia said and kissed him on his cheek and blew a kiss to me. And then Bailey Marie followed up with, "Night, Mr. Marc. Night, M. Etienne," and blew us both kisses.

"Night, you two. Get some sleep, will ya?" Laughter followed us out as we closed the bedroom door.

When we arrived back at the porch, Marc went to the linen closet for a pillow and blanket for the couch. Beau and Shell had already gone to bed, and Armand was playing keep away with Renee and her car keys.

"I can drive just fine."

"I smelled that cocoa. You must have had three or four shots in each glass."

"I'm a big girl, so I have a higher alcohol tolerance."

"Well, I'm bigger and I had half a beer, so the most sober person gets to drive. Since I'm under the legal limit, and you clearly are *not,* I drive."

"You're infuriating!" Renee told him, but she grabbed her bag and followed him out. "We're taking my car. I have work in the morning, and you don't."

"Fine, just get in the car." With that, they raced off.

I cleaned off the porch and moved chairs back in. Gelly was sitting on the porch steps snoring as she leaned against the railings. I woke Gelly up to head to her house, but ended up carrying her because she kept stumbling. I put her in bed with me where she belonged. Not that she noticed. The ladies would be hurting in the morning.

❦

23

Courting … The Morning After

Angelle

I woke up the next morning to an ear-splitting racket in my kitchen. My mouth, best not to talk about my mouth before I brushed my teeth. I opened my sliding door and quickly slid into my bathroom. I put toothpaste on my toothbrush, turned on the hot water in my shower, and let the water pound some life back into me as I brushed my teeth. I rinsed my mouth to get rid of the God-awful taste I had in there. When I turned the shower off, stepped onto my fluffy Hello Kitty rug, and slid on my long silky robe, there was a knock on the bathroom door.

"Yes?" I said, winding my hair up in a hair turban.

"Coffee?"

"God, yes!" Etienne slid open the door and handed me a large mug of coffee. The mug said, 'I like my coffee like I like my humor, dark and bitter.'

"Nice mug. I made your coffee, like you like it." I took a big swig and enjoyed the creamy, sweet coffee.

"I'm glad you understand irony. This is perfect. Ah … we didn't do anything last night, right?"

"Gelly, you were three sheets to the wind. I put you to bed, gave you some water and aspirin, and later in the night, helped you throw up." He slid the door closed and stomped back to the kitchen area.

"I figured, but I had to ask," I yelled through the door. When I had finished my morning ablutions, I stepped out and saw that he was sitting at the table drinking his coffee with two plates of food on the table. I sat across from him. "I'm new at this, you know. Haven't dated anyone since high school."

"If any high school boy had sex with you when you were drunk, I would need you to tell me his name." He handed me a plate of fried eggs and toast smothered in butter.

"Why, so you could arrest him?" I took a bite of my eggs and followed up with a bite of toast. "Why is this so good?"

"Grease, it's better than hair of the dog … which is a myth, by the way. You can't drink yourself out of a hangover. Eat some more." He motioned to the plate. "So, any former beaux I need to know about?"

"There was only ever, Alex. Nobody messed with me because I was a Babineaux and had two gigantic brothers and he was a Landry and had a gigantic family … as you know."

"Our family is prolific. We like kids." He paused for an instant. "Do you like kids, Gelly?"

"Is this how you're going to court me? Because you're terrible at it."

"Am not."

"Are too."

"Am not." We could hear the Littles chuckling outside the door at our badinage.

"That's it. I'm going to get an outsider's objective opinion." I pulled out my phone, looked up a number, and called it, walking out to the porch. "Tante Clothilde! *Comment ça se plume?* [How are you?] *Bien, bien.* I have a question for you. Do you think a man should ask a woman if she wants kids before he asks her out on a date?" I listened for a bit. "Of course, I like children. Yes, I want children, that's not the point.

Yes, technically, we've been dating for a while. Yes, I'll put you on speakerphone." I was starting to think this was a bad idea. Etienne made a 'what were you thinking' gesture as he joined me on the porch.

"Etienne, *cheri*, what's going on over there? I heard you and Gelly got into a mess at her new dance school."

"It's all over, Nanny. Gelly and I are both fine, and the bad guy is no longer amongst the living."

"When are you two getting married? I gave you that ring over a month ago." Etienne dropped his head and shook it while I snickered.

"I haven't asked her yet, Nanny." His hand went to his pocket.

"Well, why the hell not?! Neither of you are spring chickens anymore."

"That's a special ring, Etienne. A ring of true love. My Henri gave it to me when we wed."

"You were married?"

"For all of six months. Henri was a sailor, died in Korea six months after we wed. You and he were a lot alike. Both sailors, both with big plans. When he got out, he wanted to join the FBI as well. It was new back then."

"Ahh," I whispered, "That's sweet."

"Now tell me again why haven't you asked that girl to marry you? You've been dating her for months."

"We aren't there yet, Tante Clothilde," I told her.

"Don't you love each other?" There was silence on the line as Etienne and I looked at each other.

"Did this damn phone break again? I swear I hate these stupid cellular contraptions."

Etienne answered her, "I do love her, Nanny."

"Did you tell her?"

He cleared his throat. "In a manner of speaking."

"What the hell does that mean?"

"It means that he yelled at my brother that he loved me during a fight," I told her helpfully.

"I'm sorry Gelly girl, I apparently raised an idiot. I'm sure when you told him you loved him, it was much more romantic."

Etienne scoffed, sat on my porch bench, and crossed his arms over his chest. "Hardly!"

"Well, now, it had been a while for her, Etienne. You need to give her the benefit of the doubt."

"She yelled, 'Why do I love you, you idiot?' to me." Etienne told her.

Not wanting Tante Clothilde to think badly of me, I added, "I yelled it as he was finally unlocking his patrol car door and letting me out. He kept me prisoner in there for over an hour!"

There was silence on the line as Tante Clothilde absorbed this. Then we heard clapping on the phone, as Tante Clothilde called out, "I told y'all she was perfect for him. They are the perfect *couillon* for each other."

"Nanny Clothilde? Who else is there?" Etienne asked.

"Just the tanties. We are having *une tasse de café sur ma galerie*. I need to go now. Porch coffee gives us ideas, and we have some planning to do." With that, Nanny Clothilde hung up.

I bit the inside of my lips, and Etienne cocked his head at me. "Why do I have the feeling that the planning involves us?"

I let loose and hooted. "I love the tanties, but I expect when I do decide to agree to marry you, there'll be very little planning for us to do. Of course, you would have to ask for me to accept." Etienne got down on one knee, and I whacked him on the back of his head. "Not here and now, you clod. Like you've been coerced! You are impossible! Why do I love you?" With that, I turned, flung open the door, and slammed it behind me.

"One of these days you are going to say, 'I love you,' to me softly and not yelling it as a question," Etienne called through the door. I growled and flung a throw pillow against said door.

Then I heard him whisper, "I love you, Gelly, with all my heart." He turned, stuck out his tongue to the Littles and Sofia that had been watching the whole discussion and were now helplessly giggling, and left in his car.

24

Dance School

Angelle

Each day after that for the next week, Etienne met me at the door when I was ready to leave. He called it courting, but I was pretty sure it was more akin to babysitting. We would alternate going to breakfast at Myran's and the Soleil Café, where we would talk about our day and assiduously avoid any discussion of marriage or love. Then he would drop me off at my *Danse avec moi* studio to prepare for my upcoming big opening.

Every day someone met me at the studio to 'help me' with finishing touches. Again, code for babysitting. Most days it was Armand, because he was off on leave. Today was the last day to prepare. Our first dance class was tonight, and the open house was tomorrow.

"Good morning, Gelly. What's on your agenda for today?"

Pulling out the white board that I purchased, I said, "Right now, I'm making a weekly agenda of available classes. Later, I'll create a pricing plan I can post for individual, unlimited, and one to five times a week classes."

Armand scrunched his face. "That doesn't sound like anything I can help you do. How can I help?"

"Once I get the agenda and pricing plans completed, I'll need you to attach them to that brick wall behind the registration desk." I pointed to the tape outline I had made on the wall.

Armand grinned. "Watch out, you're getting to be as organized as Shell. And while you are working on all that, what can I do?"

With my chin, I indicated the back of the studio. "Make sure the dressing rooms are ready with paper towels, toilet paper, and that everything looks clean."

"Your wish..." and with that, Armand headed to the back of the building. He made a detour when he got halfway across the room and went and locked the front door.

"Babysitter," I whispered under my breath.

"What's that?" Armand asked, pretending he hadn't heard me.

"Nothing." So, it went all morning long, until someone banged on the front door. Startled, I looked up to see Etienne with a Lunch Box Café bag.

"Excellent!" I said and called back to Armand to come and eat.

"Ready for your big day?" Etienne asked, kissed me on the cheek, and set the food down on the reception desk.

"I'm not sure. I'm trying to think through everything."

Etienne smiled and pulled a notepad from his back pocket. "We'll make a list and—"

"—Sweet," Armand interrupted. "Which one's mine?"

"The one cleverly disguised with the name Armand on it," Etienne deadpanned.

"*Couillon*!" Armand turned to me and said, "Don't give in to his demands right away, Gelly. Make him work for it."

I snorted as he grabbed his bag of food and walked to the back of the studio.

"I'll be eating out back. Etienne, come get me when you leave for work."

I reached over Etienne and pulled out my grilled shrimp salad. "Must eat now! *J'ai faim*. Did you order the fried shrimp?"

"Of course." He deposited three fried shrimp into my salad. I took the side lemon he gave me and squeezed over the entire salad, avoiding the fried shrimp. Moving to the middle of the dance floor, I crossed my legs and sat down.

"You have blue cheese dressing in that bag of yours?"

"Maybe, but it'll cost ya."

I pouted. "Cost me what?"

With a *canaille* grin, he said, "A little sugar."

I rolled my eye, shaking my head. Then I got up, gave him a chaste kiss on the cheek, and swiped a blue cheese dressing packet from his bag. Returning to my place on the dance floor, I patted the spot next to me. "Come see. Did you get yourself some fries and bread pudding?"

"Yes, I got 'myself'," he did air quotes, "some junk food for you to sample." He grabbed his bag, crossed the studio, and made his way down to the floor beside me, which was harder in his deputy's uniform.

I sniffed, but my mouth canted up. He knew me well. "It's for you too. I'm just having a few bites."

"Yes, I know, three to be exact. Now eat up. I have questions to ask you and I don't want you to be hangry when I'm asking them."

We ate as I listened to the music for my dance numbers. When I had eaten all the 'good stuff' from the salad, a.k.a., the shrimp, the cheese, and a smidgen of vegetables with each bite, I put my salad aside and dug into his fries.

"Any cancellations or issues because of the *incident*?"

"Doesn't appear to be. No one's asked for a refund or said they won't be here for our grand opening. I've been working on my introductory dance. I'm taking it from the dance I did right before the attack, because I refuse to taint any dance with fear."

"That's my Gelly. Now, I have my notepad. Talk to me about what you have left to do, and I'll make you a checklist."

"I hate making checklists."

Etienne waggled his brows and shook his pen. "I know. That's why I'm making one for you. You just tell me about all the things you've left to do."

I let loose and talked about all that was left to do, from checking emails from prospective students and parents, to making sure the windows were clean, to calling Ms. Emma and other vendor to make sure they would be there for the open house. When I was done, Etienne leaned over, kissed me on my scarred cheek, and handed me the list.

"This is great! Thank you."

"Now that I'm on your good side, let's talk about where you want to go to dinner tonight so that I can ask you to marry me."

"Etienne, I really can't think about that now right now. I have to prepare for my first dance class and for the open house." I waved my new list at him.

"Dinner then? After the class or after the open house? We can do that tonight or tomorrow night? Whatever time works for you. I want you to be able to decompress. Then we talk, right?"

"Yes, we'll talk then. You choose the place and day, as long as it's after tonight's class and tomorrow's open house."

Etienne nodded and gathered up the takeout dishes to throw them away.

"Put the cardboard in the compost out back," I told him.

He smirked and whispered, "My little tree hugger." Then he called Armand back in to watch over me.

"You engaged?" Armand asked me.

"Nope."

"Excellent, you didn't give into that non-existent Benoit charm."

Etienne flipped him the bird as he walked out of the studio, and I chuckled.

By three in the afternoon, when the first of my students began to arrive, Armand left, and Marc arrived with Sofia in tow.

"Sofia, head to the back. Ms. Emma is selling the dance uniforms that you'll need. Get yourself a leotard, tights, and ballet slippers. You can choose either black or pink."

"Black!!" Sofia said and ran to the back.

"That's my little goth." Marc smiled, his eyes following her. Then he looked over at me. "How're you doing?" He hugged me and kissed me on the head like a child.

I rolled my eyes. "Good. Ready to get things started. Speaking of which. I'll just add the uniforms to your account. We will also have dance recital outfits later on. You know tutus and such. I can make sure she gets a black one. Do you want to pay all at once, or in monthly installments?"

"Excellent! She will look adorable in her little goth tutu. Let's settle all at once."

I noted Marc's selection on my notepad. "We have parent seating over there behind the tinted glass. It's so the dancers aren't distracted. For now, go on back to Ms. Emma. When Sofia is dressed, she'll come out and you can tell her how lovely she looks."

Marc stayed halfway between the dressing rooms and me. He was clearly there to shield against any potential problems, and no doubt on Etienne's orders. I shook my head and greeted my other parents. Shell arrived with Val, Bailey Marie, and Tanner.

"I don't want to dance! That's for girls!" Tanner announced to anyone that would listen to him.

"You know, Tanner. A lot of professional ball players train in ballet," I said as I walked him to the back. Ms. Emma also had a uniform of black biker shorts and white tees. "In fact, ballet helps them with their balance, flexibility, and strengthens their joints, making them better athletes less prone to injury."

"Is that true, *parrain*?" Tanner asked Marc.

"Absolutely," Marc nodded. "Rob Gronkowski has been taking ballet since high school to get him in top shape."

"Gronk! No way!" Tanner was in awe.

"Yes, way," Marc responded. "I'm a little insulted that you would doubt my football expertise. Look." He pulled up a few articles on his phone to show him.

"Well, ok then." Tanner nodded and headed to the back. *Cher, he sounds just like Beau.*

I directed the students who arrived on the parish bus to Ms. Emma and arranged for some mothers to stay in the back, providing help and making sure my little dancers knew how elegant they looked.

By 3:30, I had all my little dancers ready.

The first dance class was a resounding success. I was nearly jumping out of my skin. Based on the number of students, I knew that Ms. Emma had sold out of all her dancing apparel. I had planned three dance exhibitions before I began class: one with the Louisiana University dancers that would be collaborating with me as instructors, another with a local Cajun/Zydeco dance instructor hired to assist with the ballroom and local dance classes, and finally, a solo performance that I had choreographed before Ray's attack. I refused to let *vauriens* clip my wings—useless people would *not* control my life.

After our exhibition dances, I called my students to the floor. Then I asked them to each move to one of the colored dots affixed to the dance floor, which would be their place for each class. Then, my dream began.

"Alright, thank you everyone for joining me in this dance. Tonight, I'll go over the major positions, and then you'll learn a dance I choreographed just for you. Y'all will get a guide after class to help you remember the positions and the dance steps. Ready?" I nodded to the pianist.

And just like that, my dream became a reality. We learned our positions, our port de bras, along with steps and kicks and turns. By the end of the class, they had it down. When their parents began clapping, I taught them all to curtsy or bow.

The class was a resounding success. I let the parents know that there would be an open house tomorrow that would include more examples of dance by my instructors. In addition, there would be refreshments, prizes, and local artists selling dance-themed jewelry and paintings.

When I finished, Shell ran up to me. "That was amazing. Did you see my kids dancing? Tanner jumped the absolute highest!"

"He absolutely did. I'm so happy you came." I hugged her.

"Beau is waiting outside. He's taking us to Myran's for celebratory shakes. Do you want to meet us there?"

"I have to clean up and settle accounts with Ms. Emma, rain check?"

"Of course," Shell hesitated. "Marc, can we take Sofia with us for shakes while you stay here?"

Clearly all my friends were in on the 'Protect Gelly' machinations. I smirked at Shell. "Um hum."

"Well, gotta go. We'll see you when you get home." She gathered up the kids and headed out before I could scold her.

"What do you need me to do?" Marc asked me.

I folded my arms over my chest and told him. "I know what you're doing."

"Helping. I'm just being neighborly."

"Babysitting. You're watching over me."

Marc shrugged. "It might take Etienne a while to recover from seeing you with a gun to your head. Actually, he might never recover. You're going to have to humor him on this one."

"He can't always protect me!" I said as I cleaned up the parent area.

"I can try," Etienne said as he walked through the doors. He made a beeline for me and gave me a swift kiss on the mouth.

"Oh, yeah. I'm outta here. See you later, alligators." Marc grinned and sauntered out the doors.

"Where were we?" Etienne asked and kissed me deeply, his hands skimming my back and then cupping my ass. From right beside us, we heard a throat clearing and turned to see Ms. Emma.

"I'll just settle with you tomorrow, dear. You and Etienne have an enjoyable night." Etienne put his forehead on mine and laughed.

25

All the Feels

Etienne

I watched in awe as Gelly did her solo performance again for the open house. She told me it was the dance she rehearsed right before the attack. It almost hurt to watch it. She just opened her heart up, and I could barely breathe. I knew for sure then that she loved me. Her dance was a warm blanket on a winter's day. As she danced, her eyes met mine and after the dance, she walked to me.

"That was beautiful, Gelly. I love you!" She smiled at that.

"Now, that's more like it. I love you right back, Etienne Ulysse Benoit."

"Ulysse!" Armand said, having overheard us. Renee stabbed him in the ribs with her elbow.

Etienne smirked. "I see you've been talking to Nanny Clothilde."

"She wanted me to know, so I wouldn't be surprised when Father Lebrun said your full name at the altar."

"Does that mean you'll marry me?"

"I don't know. You haven't asked yet." When I went to go down on one knee, she turned and smirked over her shoulder, "Not yet," and sauntered away to help with the class sign ups.

"Make him work for it, Gelly!" Marc called out, and the attendees laughed and applauded.

All the instructors had sign-in sheets, and after parents and adults signed up for their classes, they headed to the registration desk to set up their class schedules and billing. The open house ended at seven, but Gelly was there until eight, finishing the scheduling. After that, she was glowing!

"Did you see how many people signed up?" she asked, then locked the studio door. "I know it was a risk to share profits with the dancer instructors, but the other studios just pay them by the hour. So, what's their motivation to be the best if they get paid the same regardless of output? My way, they're motivated to create interesting classes and recruit more students. The more students in their classes, the more they get paid."

"Communists, getting paid the same regardless of your output. I like your system better, Gelly!" I led her to my Power Wagon and opened the door for her. She got in and waited for me to close her door. Once I ran around the truck and got in, she continued to chatter excitedly.

"I know, based on the registration fees alone, I can pay my lease *and* insurance. Then I make half of their fees, while the instructors keep the other half. They'll stay motivated to recruit and retain students, don't you think?"

"You're such a savvy businesswoman." I started the truck and drove to our destination.

"Truthfully, it wasn't my idea. I went to research small businesses at the library and Kayleigh sent me to the Small Business Association. My advisor there suggested that approach to keep me from having to infuse too much cash into the business. It's a little like the Uber model, except a lot more earning potential for master instructors."

"Great idea or 'bunny day' as Shell says!" Académie, Shell's French Immersion school, used the term 'bunny day' for good ideas because they sounded like the French term for a good idea, *bonne idée.*

"Hah. *Bonne idée* indeed." Gelly grinned and looked out the window. "I thought we would be too late to get dinner somewhere. Where are we going?"

"Just a little place on Wilderness Trail." I kept my eyes on the road.

"There's no restaurant on Wilderness Trail."

"Nope."

Gelly smiled. "So, an adventure."

"Hopefully, your best one yet."

"Excellent." Gelly pulled out her phone, hooked up to the Bluetooth and started playing *Vincent Black Lightning,* by Richard Thompson. Since falling for Gelly, I, like Mr. Thompson, always believed red hair and black leather were the best color scheme.

We pulled up into a giant RV park, Wilderness Trails RVs. Gelly cocked her head as I parked in front of a giant 5th wheel RV. I went around the car and opened Gelly's door with a flourish.

"Your dinner awaits."

Gelly got down and looked over the trailer. "This is the weirdest place for a date. Whose trailer is this?" She stepped up into the trailer and gasped with pleasure. I'd set the dining room table with electric candles and my elves had recently plated the dinner.

She reached down and felt the plates. "Still warm. You had help with this adventure."

"I did. Your mama cooked, and Ms. Ellie Mae set everything up."

Gelly grinned and gave me a big hug. "This is the perfect celebration. I'm starved, let's eat."

"First a tour." I gave her a quick tour of the cozy and spacious RV with a master bedroom, one and a half bathrooms, and four bunk beds. I shrugged, "For guests, or whatever."

Gelly blinked a few times, opened her mouth, and then shut it. I took her confusion as a good sign. We ate our dinner, which included all of Gelly's childhood favorites: rice and gravy, fried okra, creamed spinach, and then she tasted what was in her wineglass.

"This is root beer! Homemade root beer!"

"Straight from the Zatarains bottle." I smiled and took a sip.

"This is the best! What's for dessert?" She bounced in her seat, excited to hear what was next.

"Graham cracker crust, a layer of banana slices, cream cheese and Cool Whip, and ..."

"Blueberries on top! Mawmaw Babineaux's blueberry and banana pie!" She danced in her seat.

I placed the whole pie in front of her and gave her a fork. In the middle of the pie, a white flourish on a blue background, was a spoonful of Cool Whip and on that Cool Whip was my Nanny Clothilde's ring. Gelly stared in silence at the ring and then gazed at me. I had pulled up a chair next to her and took her hand.

"Gelly, listen to me. I love you, and because I love you, I will do what it takes to make sure your dreams come true. Even if it means giving up on mine."

"I don't want that—"

"—Listen, whatever it takes. I need you in my life. I can't breathe when I think of my life without you or with you just in the periphery. You have to be front and center in my life, the leading role, the prima ballerina."

"Aww ... You even have a dance reference. You haven't asked yet, not that I'm complaining. You're doing a great job. I just think—"

I put a finger softly over her lips. "I'm asking you to be my wife. Whatever it takes. This trailer is ours. It will go wherever you need to make sure your dreams come true."

"And I'm saying yes and also saying if you quit on your dreams, I will kick your *t'tchu*. Which is a shame because you have such a nice little ass. Why do you think I went with cost-shared lessons? If I get a manager, I don't have to be there every day. We can go where your job takes you, and I can come back and work with the students on the fun stuff like recitals and Mardi Gras dances and such. The girls and I already worked out the logistics for everything, except where we would live when you got your job."

"And this trailer solves that problem."

"Exactly." She pulled the ring out of the pie, licked off the frosting, and put it on her finger. Then she dug her fork in the pie and lifted it to my mouth.

"Taste, you won't regret it."

"I won't regret anything with you!" I took a bite.

26

NOLA Christmas Wedding

Angelle

It took some doing to wrench the wedding from St. Francis in Meauxville to the Monteleone *en ville*. However, since that was where we first realized our love, and because the hotel was giving us an amazing discount if they could use some of our footage, Etienne and I got our way and the tanties backed off.

Renee, Shell, Kayleigh, and I were sitting in the back of the streetcar looking at the astounding St. Charles Street Christmas decorations. Andrée, the daytime persona of our 'magic night' limo driver, told us the latest *on dit* about the different families that lived in the homes. After the streetcar, we received our secret tickets to the Vampire Absinthe Bar that overlooked Bourbon Street, and we planned to spend our time people-watching before we headed in.

"What are the boys up to?" Renee asked.

"Oyster bar and beer at Deanie's Restaurant," Shell told her. "He better not smell like vomit tomorrow. I'm a sympathetic vomiter. That would ruin my bridesmaid dress."

"Ew ... TMI, I don't want to hear about that," Kayleigh grimaced.

"I thought you were an EMT. They are supposed to have strong stomachs," Renee teased, and took a big gulp of her cocktail.

"She is an EMT. Plus, she's managing my studio in the afternoon after her library gig. She's a renaissance woman." I sipped at my cocktail and smiled at my friends. I had on a sleeveless blouse and my hair was up in a ponytail. I had been stopped a number of times today by wayward drunks asking about my scars.

I just turned to them, smiled, and said, "I saved three kids' lives in a fire."

Shell always added, "My kids' lives." The *mal élèvé*, rude person, would then either say that was 'cool' or would walk off defeated because their bullying backfired on them. I looked at my watch. It was 9 pm.

"Enough of this. I want to dance with my fiancé." I texted the boys to meet us at Fritzel's Jazz Club. We had the band play *Every Day Is Not The Same* by Carol Fran and Clarence Hollimon. The song that we had danced to the last time we were Fritzel's dancing in the Crescent City. At the end of the night, we walked Andrée to her car, and then we all walked back from the club to the hotel together.

"Well, I need to head up. My mom is watching Sofia for me." With that, Marc headed down to his room.

"We'll see you all in the morning," Shell told them. She grabbed Beau's hand and pulled him to the elevator.

"Bridal suite at 11 am, bring your dress," Renee called out like a responsible Maid of Honor.

"I'm so excited!" I said and made Etienne spin me around. And right on cue, the receptionist put on Dr. John's *Basin City Blues*. I waved at them and grinned widely as Etienne spun me around and we were transported back to our magical dance of love.

"Should we be watching this?" Renee asked.

"Aww, it's so romantic." Kayleigh pulled out her phone and started recording.

When we finished, the entire lobby clapped, and I hid my face in Etienne's shoulder. Meanwhile, Etienne was hamming it up. He pulled away from me and lifted his eyebrows in expectation. I laughed and did an elegant curtsy for my adoring public. We got in the elevator and blew kisses at our audience. The elevator door closed on our laughter.

When we got to the bridal suite, Etienne pushed me up against the door, cupped the back of my head with his hand, and pulled me in for a mind-numbing kiss. He moved away, gently nipping at my lips.

"Shall we?" he asked.

I was about to say, "Please," when the door to my room flew open.

My mama was standing there in her PJs. "Not yet, Etienne. She's still my baby for one more night." Mama shooed Etienne away. I bit my lip when I saw his dejected look.

"*Demain, mon amour*," I told him, because tomorrow was the day.

T he bridal suite was pure chaos. The bridesmaids were in their skivvies and getting their hair and make-up done. I was already putting on my dress with Emma and my mom helping me.

The wedding planner, Sylvio, came in to announce, "We are on time. The groomsmen and the groom have already taken their photos, and the photographer has taken pictures of the cake and venue. One hour, ladies, and then we need to go down."

"More champagne, please," Renee said.

"No, you are cut off. We need you walking down the aisle, not falling." Renee was about to complain about how high handed the planner was, but it wasn't her big day. So, she shrugged philosophically and took a plate of fruit instead.

"Can I have another glass, Silvio?" I asked.

"How many have you had?"

"Only one, but I set it down, and it got warm, so less than one." Silvio put an apron around me and poured me another glass.

"Just one, and you can all have another half glass once you are all done with hair, make-up, and your dress styling."

"Excellent, then we each get a half glass for Denise and myself," Ms. Ellie Mae said in her soft drawl. A clear indication she had been raised in the North, that is north of Alexandria, Louisiana. She handed a glass to my mama, and they watched the other girls scurry around getting ready so that they too could earn their half glasses of champagne.

"Like mice in a maze," my mama said and then she raised her glass to Ms. Ellie Mae.

"*Santé!* Cheers!" Ms. Ellie Mae said, as they clicked their glasses together.

"We're gonna find the men and make sure their ties are all on straight," Ms. Ellie Mae told the group.

"In thirty minutes, we need you in the ballroom for pictures," Silvio barked.

"We'll be there," my mama told him and they went to find the *boys*.

We tracked them all down twenty minutes later. The groom and the groomsmen were on the rooftop deck by the pool, enjoying one last beer before the ceremony. I hid in a corner, out of sight, while my mama and Ms. Ellie Mae corralled them all.

"They're a handsome lot!" Ms. Ellie Mae said. I had to agree, as I peeked around the corner.

"Two down," I heard Mama say.

"And two to go," Ms. Ellie Mae winked back at her.

The mamas scolded the men for being so close to the pool and then secured promises that they would head down in ten minutes for pictures. Mama grabbed Ms. Ellie Mae's arm, and we all headed to the ballroom for pictures.

Once the pictures were taken, the guests began to arrive. The groom and his best man, Armand, went to stand at the front of the church. Armand having gotten the position of best man by losing at Call of Duty. Tante Clothilde and the tanties were all in the front row with my mama, watching their plan come to fruition. While my daddy, my bridesmaids, and the groomsmen waited for the music in the back with me. Shell walked on Beau's arm. Renee was paired with Marc, and Kayleigh was paired with Renee's brother, Jeb, who had just arrived that morning on leave from the Army.

My Daddy and I waltzed down the aisle to *Mon Papa* by Buckwheat Zydeco, making the father-daughter dance part of the ceremony. When I arrived at the front of the church, Daddy kissed my wounded cheek and then placed my hands in Etienne's. He gave Etienne a very stern look before he went to sit down. Etienne, too, kissed my cheek. Then he held my hands as we turned to Father Lebrun, who began the ceremony in French.

"*Mes chers amis* ... My dear friends ..."

After the ceremony and the pictures, when it was time for the maid of honor and best man to make a toast, Renee got up, raised her glass, and said, "Words aren't Gelly's thing. She's more of a doer, and in that vein, we give her a dance. Bear in mind, we're not all dancers, so we might need some help with this one. To you, Gelly, we love you!" At that moment, Renee, Kayleigh, and Shell started to do the Freeze to Ronnie

Milsap's, *If You Don't Want Me To*, a Louisiana PE staple. Within minutes, I had run down, dragging Etienne behind me to join in the dance.

When it was done, Armand, as best man, took the microphone. "I'm not a talker,and I'm not going to reveal every dumbass thing Etienne has done in his life." Soft chuckles were heard throughout the attendees. "I'll say that Etienne is solid as a rock and that Gelly can rely on him, but Etienne, you're going to have to dance a lot more in your life, and that's a good thing. With that in mind, we have an easy one for you. We'll even help you with it."

They pulled him down to the floor and they started doing the line dance to Rockin' Sidney's *Don't Mess With My Toot Toot!* I was giggling as the boys hammed it up, slapping their butts when Rockin' Sidney sang about slapping behinds, and raising their fists when he threatened to break someone's face. At this point, I was giggling so much my stomach hurt. When they finished, I hugged all the groomsmen and gave Etienne such a kiss that it merited a standing ovation.

After the meal, my daddy walked up behind my chair, gave me his hand, and *Mon Papa* by Buckwheat Zydeco began to play again.

"They're playing our song, *mon ange*. You will always be my angel." We danced again with my head on my daddy's shoulder.

"I thought it would be easier this time. Giving you away again, but it never gets easier."

"*Je t'aime papa pour toujours.*"

"I know. I'll always love you, too, but I also know you will be headed off to God knows where with your FBI fiancé."

"Husband," I corrected.

"I know, and you need to know that you will always have a home with us."

"We're keeping the tiny home there, Daddy. I'll come back often for dance school recitals and special events, to make sure everything is running smoothly."

"You do that, and here." He pinned five one hundred-dollar bills on my dress. A Cajun tradition to give the newlyweds a good financial start. "We need to make sure that your in-laws step up their game."

"You're incorrigible! They are going to think you are showing off."

"I am. You need money for your new life, and you get to earn it in your favorite way, by dancing. *Danse toujours mon bel ange.* Always dance, my beautiful angel." At that, he kissed me on the cheek and allowed me to dance with my friends, family, and in-laws.

By the time we were ready to leave, you couldn't even see my dress. There was so much cash pinned on it.

"Looks like you have the down payment on a house," Beau told Etienne as we sipped Sazeracs at the bar.

"We already have a home. We'll use it for a college fund." Etienne told him.

"Wait, you bought a house and knocked up Gelly?" Marc asked.

"Hey, some respect," Beau said. "You don't say 'knocked up' when talking about my sister." He cuffed Marc lightly on the back of his head, nearly spilling his scotch. I giggled at the by-play.

"Fine, so you bought a house, and Gelly is *en famille*?" Marc reiterated, but in Franglais.

"We have a fifth wheel and no babies." I told him.

Etienne shrugged. "She is used to living in a tiny home, but that's a little too small for me. So, wherever I land, we'll purchase some property, set up a yard and some gardens, and be right at home."

"And the other bit." Marc sipped on his scotch and raised his eyebrows Groucho Marx style.

"No, baby ... yet. It will be up to her." Etienne smiled. "Hopefully it won't be long or I'm pretty sure Nanny Clothilde will have something to say about that."

"Hey, I get a say as well," I snickered.

"Yes, you are now the top woman to run my life."

"And don't you forget it." I walked off to socialize while Etienne hung with his Krewe.

$$\text{⁂}$$

Epilogue

Etienne

I left the Krewe to find my wife. My wife, I liked the sound of that. I found her talking to Nanny Clothilde.

"All I'm saying is, I'm not getting any younger." Gelly was squirming under my nanny's scrutiny. She took a sip of champagne to delay her response. I figured I was obliged, as her husband, to step in.

"Nanny, I'm pretty sure whatever you're talking about will need my input." I put my arm around my new wife.

"Your contribution, at any rate," Nanny mumbled. Gelly snorted champagne and started coughing. I pulled my hankie from my pocket and handed it to her.

"Okay. I think it's time for us to head up." I steered my new bride to the elevator and away from the masses. We headed back to her room. Little Monteleone elves had transformed her bridal suite into our honeymoon suite.

This time when I kissed her against her door, there were no parental surprises. We opened the door while still kissing. Kicking the door shut with my foot, I unzipped Gelly's dress while she unbuttoned my shirt. I needed to slow down to make this moment special, unforgettable. I pulled back and turned her around as I eased the dress off of her shoulders. Like opening the last Christmas present, I savored her. Another Diva confection but in celadon green lace. Fancier than the dress she wore that night, but it inspired all my memories. She stepped out of it, and I draped it over a chair before I dropped to my knees in front of her and lifted her light green slip.

I inhaled her scent and dug my fingers into her hips as I moved her closer to my mouth. I licked her core, delicately flicking her clit. She moaned.

"Now, please."

I shook my head, adding some friction to my task. Gelly moaned again, demanding, but this time I would not be so rushed. *Start as you mean to go on.* I continued slowly, building, pulling away, nibbling, blowing.

"Now!" Gelly demanded, tugging on my hair with both hands. I sucked her clit and eased a finger into her wet core. I pulled a moan, then another, and finally a groan as she crested.

She swayed toward me, and I picked her up and laid her on the bed. As she lay still, replete, I leaned over and breathed out, "Mine" in her ear. I eased the slip straps off her shoulders and tugged, but the slip wouldn't budge.

With no patience, I tore through the thin slip, just as Gelly said, "Don't you dare."

I nipped her ear and promised, "Shopping tomorrow."

With closed eyes, she smiled. "Hmm, fellatio, shopping, and sex, the trifecta." Then she opened her eyes and frowned, "Clothes. Why do you still have clothes on?"

"Working on that." I pulled out my three-pack of condoms as I tugged off the rest of my clothes.

Gelly snorted. "Glad to see you're better prepared. Three, huh?"

I grinned, flipped her over, and slapped her taut ass. She giggled and wiggled as I shoved pillows under her. I covered her and laid my head between her shoulder blades, just breathing her in, and said, "Think of it as three bites of pleasure." I took another inhale as Gelly started to wriggle.

"Get to it!" she demanded.

A chuckle shook me, and I played with her breast and fingered her, my dick pressing against her thighs until she let out a sound, something between a moan and a growl.

"My impatient hidden hedonist." I offered her my thumb to nip at as I entered her slowly. She growled and moved against me.

"Soon," I whispered, pushing forward and flicking her clit.

"Hmmph ... You're not the boss of me." Then she moaned.

I smiled against her ear. "I am tonight."

The little trickster, then gave her hips a twist. At my gasp, she snickered. *Enough torture.* I started moving in earnest, then playing with her clit as she licked and nipped at my thumb. When I felt she was on the brink, I nipped at her earlobe and ordered, "Now!" She went off in brilliant technicolor and took me along with her.

I rolled off her in catching my breath. *Together forever ... Toujours.*

As Gelly whispered my thoughts, "*Toujours.*"

If you just want to bask in that sunshiny HEA feeling, stop here!

Otherwise, read the steamy start to Renee's story.

<hr>

Au suivant [To the Next One]

Renee

"I guess the show is over," Armand said, as he watched Gelly and Etienne sneak off to their room.

"This was such a sweet wedding." Kayleigh wiped a tear from her cheek and yawned.

"Too sweet," I added, yawning as well.

"Let me walk you both back to your rooms," Armand offered, extending his arms to each of us as we made our way to the elevator. We dropped off Kayleigh first.

"You okay?" Armand asked me as we made our way to my room.

"Yeah, why?"

"You keep sighing."

I sighed again. "Weddings make me pissy."

Armand guffawed at that. "An excellent trait in a Maid of Honor. And why is that?"

"I don't know. It seems like a lot of hassle." We turned down my hallway, and my empty life loomed.

"For love?"

"Screw love, I just want a kid. The problem is, I have to negotiate love and dating and all that crap to get what I really want." We got to my door, and I turned to him. "It's a hassle that I'm going to avoid."

Armand rubbed his square jaw and said, "I think you need that step to have kids, Renny. I mean, I know sometimes women think we're useless, but if there's one act that we're essential to, it's begetting children."

I opened my door and turned around. "Not if I use a sperm donation. I'm saving up. I mean, technically, a man is involved, but I don't have to deal with the hassle of love." I started to close my door. Armand put his hand on the door, his really big hand. *How much champagne did I drink?*

"Sperm donation? What are you talking about?" He wouldn't let me close the door.

"You know, they test the donor for genetic, medical, and mental health conditions, plus I get the family and medical history of the donor, and then their sperm gets evaluated...to make sure it can do the job."

"You are going to have some stranger's baby? How much is that costing you?" he yelled.

"Shh ... Not a stranger, a sperm donor, and if it takes right away, it's only like two grand plus the procedure, so three grand ... more if I need more treatments." I tried closing the door again, but Armand was not going to let me. He still had questions.

"You're going to spend a fortune to get knocked up by some guy that you don't even know? Some guy who jizzed in a cup for money? That's crazy!"

"Will you lower your voice? Get in here if we are going to talk about this." I grabbed his arm and dragged Armand into my room. "And it's not crazy! What's crazy is waiting for years to try to fall in love, only to be met with losers and cheaters and assholes. So, at nearly thirty, with my biological clock echoing in my ears, I have no children, no relationship, and no prospects. And now, I have very little time. You know after thirty-five they call it a geriatric pregnancy ... like I'm a grandma giving birth." With a stubborn fold of my arms, I glared at him.

He lifted his hand in the international sign of calm down without actually saying, 'calm down.' "Okay, relax. Tell you what, I will donate the natural way." Why was his crooked grin so adorable?

I did not uncross my arms or relax. "Are you asking me to sleep with you?"

"I'm just saying I have all of my tests. I'm completely clean, and I can give you a kid for free."

"Not free, nothing is free. If I have your kid, then you get a say in how I raise him or her."

"That probably won't be an issue. I've got a new mission coming up. And, let's just say, I wouldn't mind making sure I have someone to carry on my name if I don't make it back."

I walked over to him and hugged him. "Don't say that. You are one of my bestest friends. I can't lose you."

"You might not. You might be stuck with me. But if not, I can't think of a better person than my Valkyrie, to raise my kid."

I punched him in the arm.

"See, the kid will have spunk, kindness, and be able to take on the world. Like you." He rubbed his arm. "He might even take after his mama and get a baseball scholarship."

"Aww ... that's so sweet." I hugged him again.

"Plus, it will be much more fun than a sperm donation procedure, I *garantie!*"

I punched him again, and he chuckled against my neck.

I looked up and looked him in the eyes. He seemed serious. "What the hell? If this takes, I've saved myself a fortune."

"Plus, I'll get some paperwork in order. If something happens, the kid will get all my benefits."

"Softie. Well, alright then. Let's get to it." I started to take off my dress.

"Hold on, will you? I need ... more. A little romance."

I scoffed. "Armand, I've known you for years. If ever there was a 'wham, bam, thank you ma'am' guy, it's you." I reached for my dress sleeves again, but he stopped me.

"Not with you, Renny. Just hand me the reins for once, will you?"

I frowned, but nodded. "Just this once."

He grinned, moved closer, and cradled my head in his hands. *Big strong hands.* Then he leaned down and kissed me. All thought stopped.

"Holy hell!"

He grinned down at me.

"Oh, no! Did I say that out loud?"

He nodded. I was mortified. He drew me in for a hug. I'm a tall woman, but next to him I felt petite.

He leaned down, kissing me again. When my thoughts emerged from the cloud, my dress and slip were pooled at my feet. I grabbed him, and we locked lips once more.

"Did someone forget who's in charge?" he asked. He lifted me fireman style and dumped me on the bed. His smirk as he studied me undoing his shirt made me want to throw a pillow at him. *But holy hell, he was gorgeous.* I'm pretty sure I didn't blurt out this time. A smile tugged the corners of my mouth as his clothes flew across my room. *Okay, this was so much better than a turkey baster.* I grinned at that, and Armand stopped.

"What's so funny? What's going through your warped mind?"

"I was just thinking," as I scanned him up and down, "that this *so* beats a turkey baster or whatever else sperm donation entailed." He covered his face and cracked up.

"You're ruining the mood," he scolded.

"I promise to be better. Here, let me help you with that." I reached for his belt.

He stepped back, unbuckling and removing his belt in one smooth move. The turkey baster comment slipped back into my head when he did that Magic Mike move. I snorted.

"That's it. I'm taking complete control." Armand, with belt in hand, lifted me higher on the bed. In an instant, he circled both my wrists with his belt and tucked the ends under the mattress. I could probably have slipped out, but why would I? Clothes discarded, except for my stilettos, which he inexplicably left on. He kissed and caressed me until I lost my wits.

He made his way down my body until he reached my core.

"That's not how you make a baby," I said. He licked and sucked until I could not think. With his finger inside me, the pressure rose.

Then he pulled back an instant before I plummeted over the edge. "You're right, this is not how you make a baby."

I groaned but pleaded for him not to stop. He moved closer, his lips against my core. With a warm breath, he asked, "Who's in charge?"

I moaned, and he asked again, "Who's in charge?"

"You dammit, stop tormenting me!" I could feel his chuckle this time as he gave me everything, and I just let go. The technicolor explosions behind my eyelids took over.

When I awoke, he was on top of me. I arched my back to feel his chest against mine. The whiff of champagne, sweat, and vetiver drifted over me.

"Don't forget the important part, Renny," he breathed in my ear as he swiftly entered me, and I began to crest again.

Three times, we made love, had sex. I remember falling asleep in the crook of his shoulder and smiling when he said, "Told you it would be more fun than sperm donation."

"I'll never look at a turkey baster the same way again." I laughed, and he kissed me. This time on my lips.

"Night, Renny." I fell asleep wrapped in his arms.

The next morning, my phone rang bright and early. I fumbled for the phone, dropped it on the floor, and noticed I was alone in the bed. I saw a folded note on the pillow and picked it up as I answered the phone.

"I'm married!!" I grinned at Gelly's joy. Then I rolled on my back, put a pillow under my tush and raised my legs ... *maybe*, I thought. "You're coming to my farewell brunch, right?" Gelly asked.

"Of course, I'm jumping in the shower and then I'll be down to meet you for brunch. We will give you a great send off on your disgustingly romantic honeymoon in Paris. Is everyone already there?"

"Yes, for the most part, everyone's holdin' up, all in one piece. Although, Armand looks worse for the wear. Etienne thinks he got lucky last night." Gelly laughed.

"Armand probably gets lucky every time he sets foot out of his house," I snarked, trying not to sound jealous. I needed to change the subject and quickly. "Am I the last bridesmaid?"

"Kayleigh and Shell are already here, but according to them, you had more to drink last night, so we wanted to make sure you had more shut eye. Come see me off, already."

"I'm on my way. I just need to shower." I rolled out of bed. When I got to the door, I saw that someone had slid an envelope under my door. On the front it said, *Sign these and slide them under my door, room 414. Expect some more papers in the mail. When they come in, sign them immediately.* After my shower, I got dressed, signed the papers and headed to the bon voyage brunch. On the way, I dropped off the papers to Armand. *Maybe this is the start of my new life.*

To read the rest of Renee's story, "Thrown into Love," use the QR code on the next page.

Also by Gigi Hodge

Louisiana L'Amour Series

Learning to Love: Book 1
Dance of Love: Book 2
Thrown into Love: Book 3
Noël in Love: Book 4
Storm of Love (Novella)
Louisiana L'Amour Omnibus

Louisiana Small Town Romance

The Magic of Chemistry

The Babineaux Brothers

Bayou Catfish

About the Author

G rowing up in French Louisiana, Gigi was always a reader. But writing also played a role in her life once she began teaching. She worked with the National Writing project as a teacher and then helped to run a program as a professor. She participated in several Nanowrimo experiences (write a novel in a month) throughout the years. However, after she retired in November 2022, she finally listened to her inner voice and challenged herself to become a published writer.

Important to note: Since Gigi now lives abroad, she often uses her writing to connect to her home and experiences in Louisiana. Most of the restaurants and food in her work are not fictional places, although some of them have closed. Go eat there ... you will appreciate the Louisiana cuisine. Coming from a French Louisiana background, Gigi also includes the occasional French word or expression. She plans to create a Louisiana French bookmark to highlight her most used Cajun/Creole vocabulary.

Acknowledgements

No author is an island. It takes a team to pull together a book. I want to thank mine. So, thanks to my beta readers, Rebecca Klug and Nicole Boudreaux whose insights have been invaluable. I want to thank Holly Schullo for giving me a free line edit, best author gift ever. I also want to thank the All Write Well team for their support and instruction to help me learn how to move from being a hobby writer into a published author.